The
Brontë Girls

Garry Kilworth
The Brontë Girls

METHUEN CHILDREN'S BOOKS

F.

A0007
2.

First published in Great Britain 1995
by Methuen Children's Books
an imprint of Reed Consumer Books Limited
Michelin House, 81 Fulham Road, London SW3 6RB
and Auckland, Melbourne, Singapore and Toronto

ISBN 0416191274
A CIP catalogue record for this title is available at the British Library

Printed in Great Britain by
Clays Ltd, St Ives plc

Contents

For Bobbie Lamming, with
admiration and affection.

'The word Father is rather vulgar,
my dear. The word Papa, besides,
gives a pretty form to the lips.'
Little Dorrit: Charles Dickens

Author's Note

In the nineteenth century the parsonage at Haworth village in Yorkshire was occupied by a clergyman named Patrick Brontë. He lived there with his four very gifted children, three daughters and a son. The daughters were Charlotte, who wrote *Jane Eyre*; Emily, who wrote *Wuthering Heights*; and Anne, who wrote *The Tenant of Wildfell Hall*. Their brother Branwell, like them, also wrote poetry, sketched and painted pictures. Branwell became a drunkard and an opium addict and brought serious debts upon the family before he eventually died of tuberculosis. Due in part to the insanitary conditions of the time and the bleak aspect of Haworth, the sisters all died relatively young.

PART ONE:

A Vision of the Island

Prologue

There were two small dark shapes in the far distance. A man was walking his dog along the grassy path on top of the dyke. Beyond these shadow puppets the river sparkled in the twilight. Around the river were the wetlands: marshes covered in a variety of salt-water plants. The sky above was shot with birds.

Instantly the figures leapt up close. Chris could even read the brand name of the man's hiking jacket, printed above the left breast pocket. The hound was an Old English sheepdog, but shorn, not hairy. It snuffled amongst the unkempt grass every few paces, seeking out the smells of rabbits and ducks.

Chris had found his father's old naval binoculars in a cupboard. Since the binoculars were very powerful, the detail he could observe was extraordinary.

Chris's attention switched to a river boat, cruising down the narrow channel of water. Someone was in the cabin making lunch. Chris could see the woman through the porthole. Using the binoculars was like being privy to secret worlds, in which the inhabitants were unaware of being observed. He saw the woman speak to someone out of sight, her lips moving without any sound reaching Chris, who

3

was at least half a mile away. Then Chris looked beyond the river, on the far side, where lay the area known as Rattan Island.

To the east was a land where shadows hunted the wind through tall grasses. At first viewing it might seem a silent place, the marshland, but a discerning ear would soon discover bird sounds, mammal rustlings in the reeds, the slither of snakes, the comic burping of frogs and many other noises. It was in fact an area full of life, but one which held on tightly to its secrets, both above and below the mire. An ancient yew tree stood like a sentinel marking the outer boundary of the marshes. Dykes, twice the height of a man, contained them within their long, snaking barrows. They were another world, the Essex salt marshes, another time.

In the centre of the island stood Haworth Farm, about which there were rumours amongst the local kids. It was said that the farmer himself was mad and kept his whole family chained to the cellar walls. Chris did not believe this story, but he did know that trespassers were very unwelcome at the farm. Chris could see notices through the binoculars – white boards on the edge of the marsh line – which warned strangers to proceed only if they had business with the owner, a Mr J. Craster. Any other persons were to KEEP OUT – or else.

Chris found the farmhouse in his lens. While he was staring at what must have been the back door, it flew open and a tall, severe-looking man stepped out into the yard. Behind him was a young woman in a pinafore dress and a little cap on her head. The girl was very pretty.

Suddenly, the man looked directly into the binoculars, as if he was aware he was being observed, and his expression appeared dark and angry. Chris whipped the binoculars down and held his breath. He quickly ducked behind the windowsill of his cottage bedroom and held the binoculars close to his chest.

'Stupid,' Chris said to himself, his panic settling once he realised how silly he was being. 'He can't see you, you dope. He's looking at something else.'

Nevertheless, Chris stayed hidden by the curtains and raised the binoculars slowly to his eyes, his heart still pattering. The tall man had crossed the yard now, to another, shorter man. They were speaking and pointing to the hedge, while the girl went into the barn carrying a basket. She came out a few moments later with what looked like some eggs in the basket. She crossed the yard to the back door and entered the house again. Chris thought she was a terrible dresser: like something out of a Cinderella pantomime.

So, thought Chris, he doesn't keep them locked up! Still, the farm was an eerie place, stuck out there in the middle of nowhere, surrounded by rivers and creeks, marshes and mud troughs. It was wild country. Chris knew that his schoolmates thought *he* lived in the wilderness, but those people over there on Haworth Farm were beyond the pale. Compared to the cottage the farm was in frontier country.

The land around the island was crazed by the Rivers Crouch and Roach and their tributaries. Barling Marsh lay to the west, Wallasea Island to the north and Foulness Island to the east and south. A sea of reeds stretched between Devil's Reach and

5

the Violet: two deep troughs of water. There were dangerous creeks, flooded at high tide and deadly mud at low tide, which had drowned or sucked many to their deaths. Only the birds and rats found secure footing in the creeks.

After a while Chris tired of staring through the binoculars and put them back in the cupboard where he had found them. The light was changing outside, becoming softer and duskier. He switched on his bedroom light and moths came in from the marsh and immediately began pattering at the window-panes, leaving their dusty wing marks on the glass. The birds swooped in after the moths. In the distance, out towards the river, a heron rose with a piece of silver in its beak.

'One day,' said Chris to himself. looking in the direction of Haworth Farm, 'I'll go over there.'

As if in answer the farm's lights, tiny little stars in the distance, winked into life.

1

'Who was the traitor?' demanded James Craster of his three daughters.

'Branwell was the traitor, Papa,' chorused Charlotte, Emily and Anne.

'Right!' cried their father. 'Branwell brought disgrace upon the Brontë household with his gambling and drinking. Young men are not to be trusted. They are fickle, empty-headed creatures, full of self-importance and forever whining about the privileges due to them. The three young women on the other hand,' he paused and smiled at his daughters, white pinafores over their dresses and cotton caps on their heads, 'after whom you were named – the three girls were studious and hard-working. They wrote magnificent novels and poetry, they drew, they painted, they sewed a fine seam . . .'

Emily interrupted this regular classroom lecture with one of her usual disruptive questions. 'But, Papa, wasn't Branwell a good artist too? And he *was* the first to have his verses published, out of all of them.'

James Craster gave his middle daughter, now fifteen years of age, a severe frown. 'Where did you learn that?'

Emily replied sweetly, 'From Mrs Gaskell's biography of Charlotte Brontë, Papa.'

James Craster stared at Emily while Anne and Charlotte held their breath. 'Emily,' he said, after a long time during which his daughter refused to be intimidated, 'Branwell *wasted* those talents, just as most young men waste their lives. There are some exceptions – Mr Wordsworth, perhaps, though his younger years were not without blemish – but on the whole it's as well to steer clear of young men altogether, which is why you have not been given a brother like Branwell.'

He spoke as if he were able to order girls and boys over the counter, rather than having had to trust to luck and nature.

Emily knew she had said enough. 'Yes, Papa.'

James Craster immediately softened. He was extremely fond of his daughters, all of them, even Emily whom he found a little trying at times. Emily had a rebellious streak which he found difficult to accommodate. Dark-haired like her two sisters, but unlike them, small, brown-skinned and compact, Emily had a restless nature. She was the tomboy amongst them, forever falling from hayricks and grazing her shins. Emily could throw a stone at a crow as hard and accurately as Dan the farm-hand. She was fiercely pretty, like a gypsy, and she bounced back immediately after both physical and spiritual falls.

'I know about young men,' said James Craster, using his trump card to win the game with Emily, 'because I was one myself – a selfish, ignorant young man. Fortunately, I was strong enough to grow out of that stage of my life, into the responsible man I am today, but sadly most young men remain foolish and undependable into their old age.

You should take as your model, your mother . . .'
He indicated Hannah Craster, sitting quietly knitting in the corner of the room in the farmhouse which had been set aside for schoolwork.

Hannah Craster was an ex-schoolteacher who now had only three pupils, her own daughters. She had once been an English Head at Crouchside High School for Girls, but on marrying James Craster, had encouraged him to buy the remote farm where she had given birth to her three girl babies.

'. . . your mother has *never* been foolish, not for one moment,' continued James Craster. 'The Lord in His wisdom sent me three beautiful daughters – gave them to me through their mother – for which I thank Him every Sunday in my most fervent prayers. He thought fit to smile on me, bless me with you three children, but He gave each of you a different personality. It is up to me to mould those personalities, infuse them with character.

'Now,' he said. 'I must get back to the farm work, so I leave you in her capable hands. I believe you are going to study Lord Tennyson's work this morning? A fine poet. A very fine poet. "Not once or twice in our rough island-story, the path of duty was the way to glory." Fine words for an island people such as we. Duty, Emily, rather than clever questions.'

With that James Craster left the classroom. He stepped out into the mud of the farmyard. He had not meant the island Britain in his last sentence, he had meant Rattan Island, on which stood the farm he had named 'Haworth'. His was in fact the *only* dwelling on the island, a boggy salt marsh hardly suitable for the purpose to which he put it.

When lessons were over Emily and Anne remained in the classroom to finish their work, while Charlotte, the eldest at sixteen, put on her coat and went out into the yard to fetch some potatoes stored in the corner of the barn. Charlotte left them whispering to each other, forming new secrets, reviving old ones. The household was a place which continually rustled with secrets. They were like scurrying, busy beetles, hidden in the rafters, beneath the floorboards, behind the wainscots. The air hummed continually with the murmurs of secrets.

The world outside was in winter's grip. The flatlands were white with hoar frost, which glared under the grey, swirling light from the great bowl of the sky. As Charlotte crossed the hard, rutted yard a small aeroplane came out of the clouds over the North Sea and followed the coastline south. Charlotte stared at this rare point of contact with the modern world.

'Probably from Rochford Airport,' said a harsh voice behind her. 'Sometimes they gets blowed over a bit, when the wind's whippin' down from Norfolk way.'

Charlotte turned to face Dan Selby, the middle-aged farm-hand, who was carrying a bucket of chicken feed to the coops.

Dan said, wickedly, 'Them's a smart jet aircraft, from Holland or Germany, I reckon. Nice new machine, if you ask me. Nothin' old-fashioned about that aircraft.'

Charlotte was unruffled. She knew if her father had heard Dan trying to corrupt her, he would have received short shrift. James Craster was a man who

10

loathed the twentieth century, seeing in it all those modern inventions he detested: radio, television, aircraft, motor cars, terrible weapons of war, diesel trains, computers.

He had said to Charlotte, 'In the nineteenth century mankind reached its highest pinnacle of excellence and I see no reason to exchange such an achievement for the cold household gods of this century – *machines*.'

Charlotte was no tattle-tale. Instead she determined to put Dan in his place herself.

'Leonardo da Vinci thought of the flying machine in the fifteenth century,' she said, bitingly. 'That hardly makes it modern, does it?'

Dan, short and stocky, unshaven, took off his flat cap and looked at the grassy interior of his headgear, as if expecting to find some kind of weapon there with which he could retaliate.

'That one's a new 'un,' he said at last. 'That one up there.'

'So is the pony trap Father brought back from Rochford the other day, but the trap too is of an old design.'

Dan flipped his cap back on his head and walked off, muttering, 'Smart alecky kids.'

Charlotte, tall, pale and a somewhat nervous girl, smoothed down her grey hand-made dress with her slim fingers and continued her journey to the barn. She knew, as did her sisters, that there was another world out there, beyond the marshes. She knew that world was full of machines and people who were alien to her way of thinking. She knew there were wondrous devices, such as the high-speed aircraft she had just witnessed flashing across the sky.

11

It did give her pause for thought sometimes, but she had no wish to be part of that world. Her parents had told her it was an ugly place and she believed them. Just as she believed that *some* young men brought ruin upon good families, though she would like to see one, if only from a distance.

There must be good, wonderful men in the world, she thought, though they be rare and hard to find and she did not really want to find one.

She collected the potatoes and took them to the kitchen at the back of the house, where she stood at the sink and began peeling them. Later her sisters would come and prepare other vegetables for the evening meal. Mother would cook it, as usual, with a little help from Charlotte. They had a well-ordered routine, which Charlotte liked. Charlotte preferred regularity to surprises. Unlike Emily, she detested change of any kind.

Later, when Anne and Emily joined her, predictably Emily cried, 'Oh no, not the *onions* again. I *hate* peeling onions. They make your hands smell horribly.'

'I'll do the onions for you, Emily dear,' said eleven-year-old Anne, sweetly. 'You do the carrots for me.'

'I think Emily should do the onions,' said Charlotte primly. 'It is your turn after all, Emily *dear.*'

'You would say that, Fanny Price,' snapped Emily. Emily had nicknamed her sister after the sickly-sweet and exceptionally prim heroine of Jane Austen's *Mansfield Park*.

Charlotte was not easily drawn, but continued with her own kitchen tasks. Anne did the onions. Emily the carrots. The stew was finally prepared,

12

all except the meat, which their mother would do once she had finished marking their schoolwork.

Their chores done, the girls went off to read or write, paint or draw, knit or sew, but not to be idle. There was an unspoken rule, among many unspoken rules, that one should *never* be inactive. The only time they were allowed to be idle was if they were mentally composing verse. Whenever Emily wanted to do nothing at all, she simply sat on the settle below her bedroom window and stared moodily over the salt marshes, watching the herons rise gracefully from beside still waters, or the pirate gulls robbing each other, or the knots wheeling in flight above the reeds. If her mother or father, or indeed Charlotte, happened to glance in and see her *doing nothing*, they believed she was communing with the muse.

Not that Emily disliked reading or any of the other activities which which she was expected to fill her time. On the contrary, she *loved* her poetry and novels. She especially liked the romanticism of Tennyson and Keats. She loved Byron with a passion. She did *not* like Mr Wordsworth, who had been cruel to Coleridge *and* Branwell. Traitor Branwell might be, but perhaps with mitigating circumstances.

The poem by Keats which Emily loved the best was 'La Belle Dame Sans Merci'. Emily fancied herself as the powerful fairy in the poem, who had such thrall over knights-at-arms. She, Emily, was small and strong, with a desire to rule the hearts of beautiful young men, whether they were bad for her or not.

When she had ceased dreaming at the window,

she settled down to writing her own sonnet, which she knew would please her father and mother. It was about a giant – a Cornish giant – she had already written the first four lines:

When chapel steeples pierced the dying sky
And cottage lights were stars upon the ground
And taverns gave their hearts to merry sound,
Then came the Cornish Giant striding by.

Charlotte, Emily knew, was engaged in writing a novel about Leonardo da Vinci, a hero of the household. James Craster always said: 'To be a genius one must be many things – have many talents and skills, and be excellent at them all – unique. Da Vinci was such a genius – an artist, engineer, visionary, anatomist, writer – these together are the mark of the genius. Mr Trollope was not a genius, being merely an excellent writer of prose. Lord Byron was a remarkable poet, but unfortunately just that, nothing more. Genius is manifold.' So, Charlotte, the quite good writer, was attempting a novel about a genius.

Anne was drawing birds. Progress was slow on the drawings however, for Anne was often poorly, and having to be put to bed and fussed over, though the exact cause and type of her illness remained a mystery.

James Craster looked in on each of the girls as he was passing on his way to his own room. His last call was Emily's room. Unconsciously he braced himself before knocking on her door and opening it. Emily was the daughter who always asked the questions he did not want to answer. He wondered if she lay awake at night, thinking them up, in order

14

to challenge his authority in the household. He was always on his guard in Emily's presence, ready for the attack.

'Ah, good,' he said, noticing she was at work, 'how's the poem coming?'

'Very well, thank you, Papa.'

'Good, good.'

Emily asked, 'Papa, do you *never* write poetry?'

James Craster stared at his daughter for a long moment, then said, 'I'm a farmer, my dear. A very good one. I have no time to put pen to paper. I leave that to my clever daughters. Now you won't forget you promised to help your mother black the kitchen range, will you?'

'No, Papa,' sighed Emily deeply, obviously hoping she had been forgotten.

A chugging sound came from the yard and attracted her attention, making James Craster frown. The noise came from James Craster's only concession to the twentieth century.

He said, 'I've told Dan to put on the electric generator today, because the doctor's coming this evening and may want to see Anne under a good light.'

James Craster paid for visits by the doctor, whose fee reflected the inconvenience of trudging out into the back of beyond. Their only other visitor was the schools' inspector, an old friend of Hannah's from her own teaching days, who believed the girls were being educated to the highest standard. If the children were somewhat old-fashioned why surely that was a delight in today's world, where pupils were often insolent, unruly and sometimes even physically violent?

'Papa,' asked Emily, sweetly, just as her father was about to leave the room, 'will I ever marry?'

This totally unexpected question was like a cowardly blow in the face to the unsuspecting James Craster. He stared at his middle daughter for a very long time. Finally he answered her in measured, matter-of-fact tones.

'Not for a very long time,' he replied. 'You are far too young even to be thinking about such things. Your mother was thirty-three when she married me.'

'How will I meet someone,' Emily persisted, 'if we never leave the farm?'

'A woman does not go out looking for a man. If God intends you to have a husband, he will send you one,' answered her father. 'God alone brings a husband and wife together. Now think no more about it.'

When he closed her bedroom door, he slammed it shut.

2

'Hatchly, are you paying attention? What are you looking so unhappy about?' asked David Gates, the maths teacher.

The words were not spoken in an unkind way, but Christopher Hatchly bristled immediately.

'Like it or lump it,' snapped Chris.

David Gates stared at his pupil.

'See me after the lesson, Hatchly,' he said quietly.

Chris Hatchly's retort had put an edge on David Gates's temper and the rest of the morning was unpleasant for both pupils and teacher. Gates was an ex-Royal Air Force sergeant. While he did not expect total obedience, and would not dream of issuing imperious commands or maintaining discipline through fear, he was not used to outright insolence. He fumed.

When the bell rang for lunch and the rest of the class rose to leave, Chris remained sitting. Once the classroom had emptied of noisy boys, Gates went and sat on a desk near Chris's and stared down at the sullen boy. Chris glared at the desk top, refusing to look up.

'OK, what's the problem, Chris?'

'None of your business.'

David Gates went red again, but he kept his

17

temper under control. 'I think it is my business, when you disrupt my class, don't you?'

Chris looked up. 'I didn't disrupt anything.'

'When your ill-mannered outbursts upset *me*, they upset the whole room. It may seem a bit egotistical to you, but it's a fact that I'm running this show and, if I get knocked out of my stride, the whole lesson goes to pot. With a roomful of fifteen-year-old boys – suppressed energy ready to burst from them like stars and lights out of Roman candles – I have to maintain a delicate balance here. Nobody actually *enjoys* maths, except perhaps Gilgood, who's more like a walking calculator than a human being . . .'

This made Chris grin, despite himself.

'. . . so I have to make it at least palatable to a bunch of hairy warriors who would rather be outside charging around, pillaging the countryside. I can't do that if I don't get co-operation from you.'

Chris lowered his head and nodded. 'I'm sorry.'

'And you won't tell me what the problem is?'

Chris bunched his fingers into fists under the desk. He was quiet for a long while. There was a turmoil going on inside him which was threatening him with breaking down and crying in front of Mr Gates, a man he respected really. He did not want Mr Gates to see him crying, especially since if he did resort to tears, the flood would come strong and fast.

Finally, he managed to contain his emotions enough to answer truthfully. 'It's me mum and dad,' he said. 'They've got divorced.'

David Gates let out a little sigh. 'Ahh, tough. I know how you feel. It happened to me.'

18

Chris looked up. 'You got divorced?'

'No, I mean the *same* thing happened to me, when I was young – younger than you. My parents got divorced. That was in the days when people didn't do such things, so I was a freak in the playground, as well as being desperately confused – miserable. I felt like smashing the world to bits.'

Chris nodded.

David Gates said, 'You love both your parents and it tears you apart to see them split up – that's it, isn't it?'

Chris shook his head, vehemently. 'No,' he said. 'I *hate* my father. I'm glad he's gone. He used to get drunk and hit us. But he won't stay away, even now they're divorced. He keeps coming back and trying to tell me what to do . . .'

David Gates looked uncomfortable. 'Well, he is your father still – I suppose he has access – I mean, the court said he could visit you?'

Chris tightened his lips and then said, 'It's me mum. She won't tell him to go away. He just puts upon us when he feels like it. Comes in and orders us about, tells her what to do. She cries after he's gone.'

David Gates got up off the desk on which he had been sitting and said, 'Well, I accept your apology, Chris, for this morning. You'd better go to lunch now. Do you want me to take this any further? This business about your father?'

'What further?'

'Well, I could contact the welfare officer – but if there's no restraining order out, no injunction against your father visiting your home – then I doubt much can be done. It's really up to your mum, if she really doesn't like the visits, to tell your father to stay away. It sounds as if she may still have some feelings for him though, however daft that might be in your eyes. These things are not easy to control. The whole thing gets tangled and irrational.'

'She won't do anything,' said Chris.

David Gates shrugged. 'Try not to let it get you down too much, Chris. I know that's a stupid thing to say, but I can't think of anything else at the moment.' He smiled. 'Maybe by tomorrow I'll have thought of something even more stupid.'

Chris smiled, feeling better for the talk. 'Can I go now?'

'Sure, off you go. I'll see you at the next harrowing session of calculus.'

Chris left the classroom and made his way to the dining room, where he intended to eat the sandwiches his mother had made for him. His best friend, Ishwinder Singh, was sitting alone at an end table. Chris went and plonked himself down next to him and stole one of his friend's tomatoes.

'Hey!' cried Ishwinder.

Chris said, 'You don't mind me nicking one, do you? You can't eat three. I've got cheese sandwiches. I hate eating cheese without a tomato.'

'Oh, all right then.'

Ishwinder came from Thorpe Bay, the posh area of town. His father was a banker. Ishwinder's lunches were splendid banquets of – at least to Chris – exotic footstuffs. Despite these gigantic lunches, Ishwinder was forever hungry.

Ishwinder's mum and dad always welcomed Chris into their home and Chris loved to visit his friend's house which, in contrast to his own, always seemed full of light and laughter.

Chris's house was at Paglesham Eastend, a village on the edge of the marshes. It was a little two-up, two-down cottage, just large enough for him and his mother. There had been a larger house, in Rochford, which was sold before the divorce, so that his father could buy a flat in Southend. His mother's half of the money was just enough to purchase the little cottage. In order to keep them, Chris's mother worked at the credit-card offices in Southend, dropping him and picking him up each day at the Crouchside High School for Boys.

Chris said, 'Did you see *Crystal Maze* last . . . ow!' He suddenly jerked forward, having felt a pain like an electric bolt in the small of his back. It was a couple of seconds before he realized he had been punched by someone using the edges of their knuckles. He turned to see Jason Swan standing behind him, a grim look on the other boy's face.

'S'pose you think you're clever, Hatchtop?'

'What?' said Chris, rubbing his back.

'Messin' about in maths today. You put old Gatesy into a right temper with your smarty-faced backchat. Next time you do that I'll knock seven bells out of you, right?'

Chris said nothing. Jason Swan was thickly built with the eyes and brain of an intelligent shark. He ruled Year Eleven with hard fists and a cold nature. There was no compassion in Jason Swan. Once he took a dislike to a boy, as he had to Chris, he was remorseless in his attentions. He was Chris's main rival in the classroom, both of them being amongst the brightest pupils. Added to this, Swan felt he

21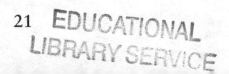

had been insulted because a girl he had been talking to after school had smiled at Chris when he passed the two of them on his way to his mother's car.

'Just watch it in future, Hatchface. Remember who's boss around here. I say what goes in the playground. Me. Got it?'

'Yeah, yeah,' said Chris, under his breath.

'Yeah!' emphasised Swan.

Two of Jason Swan's cronies called to him from the other side of the dining room and the bully gave Chris one last glare before turning away.

Embarrassed at having been intimidated in front of Ishwinder, Chris ate his sandwich in silence, his back still throbbing from Jason Swan's jab.

Ishwinder said quietly, 'It's a terrible thought, isn't it?'

'What?' asked Chris.

'It's a terrible thought that if Jason Swan had been Attila, the Huns would still be ruling the world today.'

'How do you make that out?'

'Well, Attila the Hun was just a murdering savage conqueror who showed no mercy to anyone, man or animal, laughed while he put women and puppies to the sword, slaughtered babies in their cribs, ate his own grandmother for breakfast, and threw his girl-children to the wolves, while . . .' He paused, clearly asking to be interrupted.

'Yes?' said Chris.

'Well, Jason the Swan hasn't even got *that* much kindness in his soul.'

Chris laughed out loud, spraying the table with crumbs.

After lunch the first lesson was English. Chris

managed to get on one of the computers. He had Shakespeare's sonnets on CD ROM and spent thirty minutes using the mouse to pick out the most used adjectives. Mrs Blakenely believed there were 'linchpin words, cornerstone words and keystone words', in all the works of all the great writers. She encouraged her pupils to seek out these important and otherwise disguised links in the chain of great literary works, in order to attempt to decipher the genius behind them. Chris, adept at using the computer, simply clicked on a word like *merry* and did a global search, noting all the places where Shakespeare had used that word, either as an adjective or as a noun.

Chris actually liked reading, but he knew he was unusual amongst his classmates. Most of them bought tapes of a set work and used their Sony Walkmans to listen to them while watching a school football match, or on the bus home.

After English they had games and spent the last hour of the day running around the rugby pitch, jostling each other and being jostled, while a PE teacher stood in the centre of the pitch like a circus ringmaster cracking his whip to make the horses go round and round.

When the end-of-school bell rang, Chris dashed off to find his mother's car, hoping not to run into Jason Swan on the way. He was lucky. Swan had other plans that evening. Some other youth was going to have the pleasure of the bully's company before going home.

Chris's mum was sitting waiting in her Metro. Chris opened the passenger door, threw his school bag on to the back seat, and climbed in. His mother started the car.

Sally Hatchly was a small, slightly anxious woman, with fine, wispy, blondish hair. She was thirty-three. Chris's description of how things were at home might have given someone like David Gates the impression that she was a weak woman, but this was not so. She had a core of determination a politician or businessman would have envied. She was simply still caught in the web of the past and couldn't free herself from its sticky threads just at the moment. Her confidence had taken a knock and she was wary of taking on another man.

'Good day?' she asked, pulling the car out into the traffic.

'Good and bad,' replied Chris.

'Tell me about the bad.'

'Oh, I upset Mr Gates, but we had a chat later on so that was all right. Then Jason Swan had a go at me.'

She glanced at him sideways. 'Do you want me to do something about that? He's bullied you before, hasn't he? I could go and see the headmaster.'

'No, it'd only make it worse,' said Chris, staring out of the window at the passing houses. 'It'll go away soon.'

'You're sure about that?' she asked. Then more fiercely, 'I *hate* bullies. They make the world so miserable.'

'Like Dad, you mean?' Chris said.

She was quiet for a while, as if concentrating on her driving, and failed to answer him.

'I've bought some kippers,' she said, brightly. 'We

24

haven't had kippers for ages, have we? Do you want them for tea or breakfast?'

'*Breakfast?*'

'Well, people do have kippers for breakfast – sometimes with jam on them.'

'You're kidding.'

'Only about the jam. That is, some people *do* use jam, but no one we know. So, we'll have them for tea, eh? I'll make some sauté potatoes to go with them.'

Chris stared at his mother's face, noting the little wrinkles that had appeared around her blue eyes lately.

'What?' she laughed, glancing at him again.

'You look tired,' he said, slumping back in his seat.

'I'm all right. We'll have a nice quiet evening in front of the telly, shall we? Have you got much homework?'

'A bit.'

'Well, once that's over, we can relax.'

But they weren't able to relax. Chris's father's car was parked outside the cottage when they arrived home and he was sitting bolt upright in the driver's seat, staring into the rear-view mirror, obviously waiting for them to arrive. He gave them an over-the-shoulder wave as they drew up behind him.

Chris gritted his teeth, wanting to swear and shout at the brute shape in the thick overcoat, wishing not for the first time that his father would crash his old Jaguar and kill himself on his way back to his flat.

3

'What do you want, Jack?' asked Sally, wearily, as her ex-husband got out of his car.

Chris's father hunched beneath his overcoat collar and looked hurt. 'Do I have to want something? I just came to make sure you two were all right. I do have some sense of responsibility towards my family.'

'We're not your family any longer,' Sally replied, walking down the winding path, through the small conifers and the two plum trees, to the front door of the house. 'You made sure of that when you went off with Silvia.'

Silvia had been a receptionist at the firm of solicitors next door to Jack's office. Jack was a civil servant, a Higher Executive Officer in the Southend VAT building. He was a thick-set, good-looking man with horn-rimmed glasses, whose broad face was frequently caught in a smile. He could charm a cobra with his deeply hypnotic blue eyes. Sally was still in love with him, even though she now hated him, and two such warring passions meant that Chris often heard her crying in the night, softly, so as not to wake him.

Jack said, 'I didn't go off with her. You left *me*, remember. I went to her afterwards.'

'It's just an expression. We both know why we had to separate. The violence . . .'

'That's all in the past,' said Jack.

'You went to Silvia as soon as we separated, Jack, which makes me think there was something going on before I took any action. Shouldn't you be with her now?'

'I came to see *you*,' he replied, affronted.

Jack followed them, uninvited, down the garden path to the house. Sally opened the front door with her key and pushed Chris inside, ahead of her. So far Chris had not said anything, happy to leave things to his mother. When Jack made as if to follow them into the house, Sally barred his way.

'This is *my* house,' she said.

'Aren't you going to offer me a cup of tea? What's happened to that famous hospitality?'

'It dried up,' snapped Sally.

'What do you say, son?' asked Jack, looking over Sally's shoulder at Chris.

'Leave us alone,' replied Chris. He was still afraid of his father, but was relieved he could not smell alcohol on Jack's breath. The rages Jack went into were almost always preceded by bouts of heavy drinking.

'Leave us alone,' mimicked Jack in a falsetto voice, his face clouding. 'You always were a wimp – Mummy's boy.'

Jack had managed to push his way into the front room now and was taking off his scarf.

'Just one cup of tea, then you go,' said Sally, going into the kitchen.

Jack sat down heavily in one of the armchairs.

27

Wickedly, Chris said quietly, 'Tom usually sits there – that's Tom's chair.'

Jack glared hard at his son. 'What are you talking about?'

'Mum's new boyfriend.'

Sally Hatchly had recently met a social worker named Tom Garfield. He had taken her to the Westcliff Palace Theatre, to see Arthur Miller's *Death of a Salesman* and had been round to the house twice since. The last time was a week ago, but Sally had turned down the next offer to take her out, saying she wasn't ready for a long-term commitment.

Chris enjoyed watching the expression on his father's face. He looked as if he was being probed by a sharp instrument in an open wound.

When Sally came in with the teas, Jack said, 'Who's this fellah you've been seeing?'

Sally had just put on some blue eyeliner and a coral lipstick. Her fine hair had been brushed into springing curls. She always made up when Jack came round. She told Chris this was in order to look her best, to show his father that she was doing very well without him, thank you, but Chris guessed it was also to let Jack know what he was missing. Sally had a very pretty face, which the subtle use of cosmetics enhanced.

'None of your business,' said Sally, darting a look at Chris which was supposed to shrivel him.

Jack coughed, bringing a hand up to his mouth. Chris was glad to see his father ill at ease. Jack pulled at the sleeve of his overcoat, straightening out the wrinkles, as if this were a desperately important gesture. 'I think,' he said, 'it is my business, since it involves my son. I don't want him being influenced by unsavoury types.'

'He's already been that,' snapped Sally, becoming more angry than Chris had ever seen her. 'His father is pretty unsavoury.'

Jack looked as if he had been struck in the face, but instead of retaliating, he asked, 'What does he do, this Tom person?'

Chris said, before his mother could stop him, 'He's a social worker.'

Jack laughed out loud at this. 'A social worker? Poor sap. What does he earn? A pittance, I'll bet. They're the dregs of the earth, those people.'

Sally said bitingly, 'Make up your mind. Do you want to attack his salary, his profession, or Tom personally?'

'Profession? It's a disgrace.'

'Tom,' Sally said slowly, 'is a kind, thoughtful and compassionate man. He's unselfish. In fact,' she added, 'he's everything you aren't. That's why I like him.'

'All social workers do,' spat Jack, 'is take kids away when they shouldn't, or leave them to die when they should.'

Sally smiled and shook her head. 'What a marvellous assessment of a profession. I could say that all solicitors do is take more money than they should, for as little work as possible. There are many kinds of social worker, Jack, not just those on the child protection side – who probably do a pretty good job considering their funding. They care for the elderly as well. Tom just happens to be in mental health. He helps to care for the mentally ill.'

Jack would not be turned from his prejudice.

'There was that kid in Liverpool last week – the social services let it die.'

'The child's father beat it to death. We know all about violent fathers in this household, so don't go off on that tack. The social worker in question was working a ninety-six-hour week, in order to see her clients. It was the system at fault, not the workers. You know *nothing*, Jack.'

Chris watched this exchange with some concern, noticing that his father was becoming more and more angry.

'Oh, you're an expert on social work now, are you? Since when? Since this bloke came on the scene?' said Jack.

Jack stood up and thrust his hands into his coat pockets and stared out of the living-room window. Beyond the long, narrow garden were ploughed fields, barren in the winter. Occasionally a heron alighted in these fields, surrounded as they were by creeks and ponds in the low-lying landscape. There was one out there now, being mobbed by seagulls who objected to its presence for some reason. Chris could see his father staring hard at this bird, some two hundred metres away, as if he too harboured malevolent thoughts towards the creature.

'I think you ought to go, Dad – you're upsetting Mum,' said Chris at last.

Jack whirled. 'Who asked you?' he exploded, his face puffed and ugly with fury.

Chris shouted, 'Nobody has to ask me. This is my house, not yours. Don't you come here trying to tell us what to do. You've got no say.'

Jack took a step forward, his fists bunched, but Sally suddenly came to life.

30

'You touch that boy,' she said in low fierce tones, 'and I'll have you thrown in jail for assault. You hear me, Jack? I'll make sure your name is splattered all over the front of the local newspapers. Wife-beater! Child-beater!'

Jack stopped in mid-stride, the veins in his forehead standing out like cords. He was breathing heavily. For a moment Chris thought Jack was going to strike his mother, then a trickle of reason must have found its way into his father's brain, as the fist unclenched and the shoulders relaxed.

'Where does he learn those manners, that's what I'd like to know?' Jack snorted. 'From that social worker, I expect. Haven't you been taught to respect your father and mother, Christopher?'

Sally opened the door. 'Leave,' she said. 'Now – before I call the police.'

Chris cried, 'Mum's going to get a court injunction out on you – to stop you coming here.'

Jack stared at his wife. 'Is this true?'

'Yes,' she said. 'I've had enough. You have no right to be meddling in my life. Stay away.'

'I'll get access, to him,' Jack said, nodding at Chris. 'I don't want some other man corrupting my child. Teaching him to hate his real father.'

Sally said quietly, 'Nobody has to teach him how to do that – it comes naturally.'

Finally, giving Chris a last murderous look, his father stormed through the doorway and along the path to his car. Chris didn't relax until he heard the engine die away along the country lane which led to Rochford. He and his mother both let out a sigh of relief.

A few minutes later, while they were drinking the

tea, Sally said, 'Where did you learn that, about an injunction?'

'Oh, we do that sort of thing in class – you know, law and constitution,' he replied. He was not telling the truth, but he didn't want his mother to know he had been discussing family business with one of his teachers. It might upset her.

They had their kippers for tea, then Chris did his homework, though his mind was hardly on his books. He felt trapped, like an animal in a cage, wondering if they were ever going to be free of his father. When the divorce had become final he had thought he would never see his father again. Certainly Jack had put in no request to visit Chris. Nor had he asked Chris to visit him. Jack wasn't really interested in Chris. It seemed his father was still involved with Sally though and wanted some control over her life. Jack was interested in power.

A wind was blowing over the marshes, across the river, gently rattling the panes in the old sash window. Outside it was black, except for one pinprick of light, somewhere out in the middle of the salt marshes, near Devil's Reach. That would be the farm on Rattan Island. Chris went to the cupboard where the binoculars were kept, but when he took them out he inadvertently dropped them. They crashed on to the floor causing Sally to yell, 'What's that?'

'Nothing, mum,' he said, picking them up. 'Dropped something.'

When he tried to peer through the binoculars, he found both lenses had been knocked out of alignment. He could see nothing but dark, overlapping moon shapes. Frustrated, he put the binoculars back in the cupboard. Then he went to the window and stared out at the island with his naked eyes.

'Why would anyone want to live out there, though?' said Chris to himself. 'Spooky.'

'What's that, dear?' He turned to see his mother coming through his bedroom doorway with a cup of chocolate in her hand.

'Thanks, Mum. I was just thinking about that light out there, over the river.'

'Thinking out loud, eh?'

She peered over his shoulder, through the window.

'Bit isolated, isn't it?' she said.

Chris nodded, thinking, if we lived right out there, Dad could never get to us.

Sally asked, 'Are you coming down to watch some telly?'

'Not at the moment. I'm going to play a game first, then I'll come down. Monkey Island.'

Chris had an Amiga on which he had several arcade games.

'Well,' said his mother doubtfully, 'don't spend too long in front of that thing. I'm not sure it's good for your eyes. All those glaring colours.'

With that she left and Chris took out the frustrations of the day on his computer, using his mouse to guide the screen hero through various adventures on Monkey Island. In the back of his mind he saw himself as a great expeditionary hero too, exploring the forbidden reaches of another island. One which had a strange farm where a pretty girl lived with a tall, grim-faced father. A girl waiting to be rescued.

PART TWO

Behold the Maid

4

At about the time that Christopher Hatchly was staring at the light from Haworth Farm, Emily and Anne Craster were thinking about retiring for the night.

They had mostly spent the evening, as they did so many evenings, around the piano. Hannah had been playing, while Anne and Charlotte sang a duet. Emily was not very good at singing, did not like it much, and played the piano mechanically. She had little sense of pitch or musical rhythm and, when called upon to entertain the rest of the family, preferred instead to recite poetry or prose, her clear strong voice infusing the words with relevant meaning. She was entirely capable of holding the attention of her audience. Emily was the actress, though that word was never mentioned in the house. There were seedy connotations in Craster eyes.

The girls wore their home-made evening clothes: dresses cut from dark-coloured velveteen, with removable white lace collars. Their hair was done up with ribbons. They wore plain flat-soled shoes. The girls bunched around their mother playing the piano, and James Craster stood with his back to the open fire, warming the seat of his pants, smiling with evident satisfaction upon the scene. An observer would have thought it a set from the film of *Pride and Prejudice*, just what James Craster wanted one to think.

When Hannah had finished playing 'See, the Conquering Hero Comes', she was in tears. No one mentioned this. In fact the father and daughters were talking and laughing. They all knew that Hannah was prone to bouts of melancholia and to pay attention to it would be to encourage more tears. It was such a commonplace occurrence in the Craster house that it was quietly ignored.

Then James Craster said, 'A brighter tune, I think! A Strauss waltz. Charlotte, you will dance with me, while your sisters partner each other.'

He put his arm around his eldest daughter's waist.

'No, no,' said Charlotte, demurring. 'I shall play the waltz and Mamma can dance with you.'

Hannah started to rise from the piano stool, but James Craster said, 'I insist. Play, Mother.'

Hannah seemed to hesitate, her eyes seeming to burn, but then after a moment she dutifully resumed her seat and began playing a waltz. James Craster danced stiffly and formally with his eldest daughter, staring into her face the whole while, his own expression rigid and unsmiling.

Charlotte, too, did not smile. Her dancing was a little more flexible than her father's, despite the fact that her back remained poker straight. She stared at an imaginary spot just above her father's left shoulder. In her mind she was not dancing with her father, but with some brave young man, returned from the Napoleonic Wars. Her lover – for she dared to call him that in the secret halls of her

38

dreams – wished to forsake war for the precarious life of a poet, and wanted this last dance with her before returning to the fields of Belgium to lead his men into a final battle. Charlotte could never get herself to allow him to survive that battle and saw herself remaining faithful to his memory for the rest of her life.

In contrast, the two other sisters danced freely and flourishingly, giggling the whole while, sweeping around chairs and table with their skirts swishing and their hair flying. Emily was always the gentleman and Anne the lady. This was the way they danced when they practised with their mother, after their morning lessons on Thursday. They were excited by the waltz and needed to express that excitement: not just with their feet but with their whole bodies.

When it was over, Charlotte let go of her father and said, 'Now shall I play for you and Mamma?'

'I think not, I think not. One dance is enough for an evening,' said James Craster. 'Time for your beds, girls – Anne, Emily. Charlotte, you may of course stay down a little longer, in deference to your more mature years.'

'Oh Papa,' humphed Emily, red-faced from the exertion of the dancing. 'A little longer?'

'No arguments, if you please. Kiss your mother goodnight.'

Hannah proffered her damp cheek and Anne kissed it. ''Night, Mamma.' Emily did the same but with less grace. Then the two girls kissed their father, on the cheek, and went dutifully up out of the room and up the stairs to their beds.

James Craster took his pipe from the mantelpiece

and went to his writing desk. There he began to busy himself with some papers. Charlotte waited until her mother was seated in her high-backed chair by the fire, then took a footstool near her feet. Charlotte loved sitting in her father's chair opposite her mother and no one would have stopped her from doing so, but Charlotte preferred to deny herself simple pleasures for reasons even she did not understand herself. Emily teased her sister with this, saying she was into 'renunciation' like Dorothea in George Eliot's *Middlemarch*. 'You enjoy pain,' Emily once said, going too far in a moment of viciousness. But she had begged her sister's forgiveness immediately afterwards, when she saw how much the remark had hurt her. They had kept this incident a secret between them.

Hannah Craster took out some embroidery, while Charlotte stared into the flames of the log fire. She appeared to be in deep thought.

'Is anything troubling you, Charlotte?' asked Hannah, glancing up from her work.

'I saw an aeroplane today,' replied Charlotte. 'Daniel Selby said it was probably flying from Holland.'

They spoke in low tones, so that James Craster could not hear them.

Hannah raised her eyebrows a little. 'Did it disturb you?'

Charlotte rubbed her feet, where they were becoming too hot from being close to the fire. There were apple logs in the grate and occasionally they let out a spurting hiss of blue-flaming gas which was quite dramatic.

'No, it didn't disturb me, Mamma. As I pointed

out to Daniel, Leonardo da Vinci designed an air machine. It just made me think – in the way that the passing ships make me think, when they sound their foghorns. Deep mournful notes, like cattle lost on the moors, wanting to be safe in their stalls.'

Hannah put down her work and stared into the middle distance.

'I think that's a rather nice description. What about this aircraft, though. Did it make you think of some lost creature?'

Charlotte shook her head. 'It looked lonely, I suppose – perhaps a solitary bee flying home to its hive – but I was thinking of the people inside it. What are they like, modern people?'

'There are all sorts of people out there – clever ones, silly ones, greedy ones, unhappy ones – the world hasn't changed much in that respect. What we object to, your father and I, is the worship of machines.'

'They pray to mechanical devices, Mamma?'

'They might as well. They spend hours on the sabbath, washing and polishing their machines, or trimming their lawns with them, or doing their accounts on them – just as your father is doing his accounts now, but he is using his brain and a very little help from a fountain pen. They lavish time and vast amounts of money on machines. Some of these devices – well, weapons of war – they're too horrible to contemplate. Machines have overtaken mankind. They use them for everything, from drying their hair to cutting down whole forests with them.

'Take a simple cup of tea. Machines are used to gather the tea leaves from the bushes, sift and grade

41

the tea, package it and transport it to foreign lands, to shops where a machine helps to sell the product. Even when it reaches the home, or a restaurant, machines boil the water and make the beverage. There's very little need for people out there.'

'It sounds awful,' said Charlotte. Her dark brown eyes took on a dreamy look of contentment. 'I'm glad you and Papa decided to leave the world and raise us here, out in this natural place. I love the birds here – the dunlin, the oystercatchers, the red-shanks – and I love the wild marshes, especially now, in the winter, when the reeds and grasses are white with frost. Don't you just love them, Mamma? The skies are so – so *big* and change often. Today they were full of dark, swirling cirrus clouds – the angry brow of God – and yesterday they were the pale blue of a hedge-sparrow's egg.'

'I suppose,' said Hannah, cutting a strand-end of cotton from her work, 'we may at some time have to consider losing you. You may some day wish to leave us and enter that world out there, for one reason or another.'

'Oh, *never*, Mamma. In any case, Papa would forbid it, would he not?' said Charlotte.

It sounded to Hannah as if Charlotte *wanted* to be forbidden to leave the farm, so that the decision to remain was not hers, but that of her parents. Hannah stared at her daughter for a few moments. A battle was going on inside her: a battle between being a good mother and being a devoted wife. When she had married James Craster he had extracted a promise from her to honour his desires to reject the modern world, a philosophy with which she had agreed at the time. Now that her

42

daughters were almost grown, she was not sure it was fair on them, to keep them away from the rest of society. James thought they would miss nothing by not marrying any young men the twentieth century had to offer, but Hannah did not share his utter conviction in his beliefs. This battle between mother and wife was the cause of much unhappiness in Hannah, who found brief comfort only in private weeping – the only private place she had was the bathroom.

'I'm not so sure your father can order you to remain here,' said Hannah at last. 'The laws of the land have changed since . . . well, since we have considered ourselves a family separate from those outside.'

'Have they, Mamma?' Charlotte said, with a worried look. 'But I wouldn't want to make Papa angry. He would be angry if I said I wanted to leave, wouldn't he?'

'Yes, he would,' replied Hannah honestly, giving Charlotte the reason she so desperately needed to stay.

Charlotte was silent for a brief time, then murmured, 'Please don't tell Father about Selby and the aeroplane.'

Hannah smiled. 'It shall be our *secret*,' she replied, softly.

This secret gave both of them a special moment. Later, one or other of them would share the secret with someone else, warning them of course not to reveal it to the one from whom it had to remain concealed. It was a harmless pleasure, though there were much darker secrets in the house which the carriers knew must *never* see the light.

The mother went back to her embroidery, now that the crisis was over. However, a new and more alarming one arose immediately afterwards. Charlotte had obviously been thinking a great deal about her life recently.

'Mamma, how did you know you were going to have three baby girls?'

Hannah's head came up again so fast she hurt her neck.

'What's that?' she asked, fearing a probing question on the facts of life. She had informed her two older daughters (but not yet Anne) that babies were conceived in the woman's womb when a man and his wife lay down together in the sight of God. Emily had predictably asked, 'What if the man and the woman are not husband and wife?' Then, Hannah had replied, it is a great sin. She now lived in fear of having to be more explicit in her explanations of procreation.

She bent her head over her work again, 'Whatever can you mean, Charlotte?'

'Well, I mean you named us after the three Brontë sisters, from Haworth in Yorkshire. How did you know you were going to have two more girls when I was born?'

They no longer spoke in undertones, because Charlotte wanted her father to hear her question too. Hannah bit her lip and glanced over at her husband, who now had half an ear on the conversation. He rose immediately and strolled over to the fire, stretching as if he wanted a short break from his work. He looked down at his daughter.

'I couldn't help overhearing that last question,

Charlotte, and I'm at a loss to understand why you need to know.'

Charlotte stared her father directly in the eyes and he knew by that look that only candour would serve him.

'The truth is,' he said, staring into the flames himself, 'you were not given the name *Charlotte* when you were born. It was only later, when Emily came along, that I conceived the idea of naming you all after the Brontë sisters. We were lucky with Anne, very lucky. She could have been a boy, but she was, as you know,' his eyes twinkled, 'a very adorable girl.'

'Do you think God had a purpose there, Papa?'

James Craster leapt on this with alacrity. 'Undoubtedly.'

'Then luck had nothing to do with it,' said Charlotte, with great satisfaction in her tone. 'It was meant to be.'

God had a peculiar position in the Craster household. They did not attend any church, nor see any ministers of religion, because that would have put the girls into contact with the world outside. So they held their own services, in the parlour, every Sunday morning. They prayed, they sang hymns, they read from the Book of Common Prayer and the King James Bible, according to the Anglican customs. In their own way, they were a devout, pious family, God-fearing and God-loving.

They contained their God, for themselves, not sharing Him, not sharing with others in the worship of Him. He was a personalised God, shaped to their own specifications, only occasionally taken out of the house onto the open marshland when they went

45

for a walk. Over a period of time, they had left out those parts of the services which did not interest them, and introduced such pieces which did. The sacraments were not followed because there was no ordained priest to administer them.

Charlotte was quiet for a short while, then asked her final question of the evening. 'What name did you give me – at first – before I became Charlotte?'

While Hannah had readily agreed to the idea of locking out the twentieth century, she was not now as convinced as her husband that it could do no harm to the children. He continually said, 'What can it do but to turn them into young women with beautiful minds? They will have all the accomplishments of a woman of the last century and none of those hideous modern fashions and traits.' It had seemed so simple in the early years, when the girls were in frilly frocks and bonnets, but it became more complicated as time went by. While Charlotte *seemed* to accept the situation willingly and happily, Hannah was always watching her daughters for signs of dissatisfaction or distress.

'Is it important to you?' asked her mother, afraid.

'Yes,' replied Charlotte.

James Craster said, 'You were named Sarah. Sarah appears on your birth certificate, but I later changed it to Charlotte by deed poll, when we were blessed with a second daughter.'

Their first daughter screwed up her eyes and looked thoughtful, before saying quietly, 'I *much* prefer to be called Charlotte.'

Hannah let out an audible sigh of relief, glad that it was not Emily who had carried another name at first, because she might have decided to cause a fuss.

Emily woke first the next morning. On her way past her parents' room she found the door ajar, so she peeked inside. The bed, she saw, was neatly made. Her father was probably out somewhere on the farmlands. Her mother was either making breakfast or feeding the chickens.

Emily pushed the door gently open the whole way and stepped inside her parents' sanctum. She stood for a moment in the peace of the white-walled room, smelling the starch on the bed linen, the faint odour of friendly dust on the floor and a thin cold draught of air from the ill-fitting window.

There was a patchwork quilt on the bed, which Emily herself had helped to make, and the sheets and pillowcases were of pure white cotton. In fact there was very little decoration on anything else in the room. Even the rugs were plain. There was a matching hazelwood chest of drawers and a wardrobe, a beech wheelback chair with a blue cushion and the rest was soft, delicate space filled with gentle bedroom air.

On the wall facing the window was a picture in a pretty frame with hearts around it. It was a photograph of Emily's mamma and papa taken when they were married. Hannah, attractive in an apple-blossom bridal dress, was hooked on to the arm of the tall, gaunt James, shyly peeping up and smiling into his broad, strong-looking face. He in turn was looking at the camera, but there was a hint of his having just glanced down at his new wife and there was an expression of quiet satisfaction in his eyes. Emily stared at the photograph, a picture of two people in love, and she wanted to clasp it to her own heart to imbibe some of the warmth of that far-off love.

This was a private place and not to be entered except by invitation. Emily had not stepped into the room for several years, but today she felt compelled to see it for some reason. She felt the hallowed atmosphere of this room in her soul. It was a spiritual place. Silent and undefiled by the meanness of the real world beyond the farm. Over-looking the bed, illuminated by the silver light from the dormer window, was a crucifix. Christ looked down upon the place where her mamma and papa slept side by side.

A small sound downstairs made Emily start, guiltily. She left the room and went down to help her mother with the breakfast and also the pre-parations for lunch.

'Did you sleep well?' asked her mother, straightening Emily's cotton cap.

'Yes, Mamma. I dreamed that Lord Byron asked me to be his wife – and I accepted.'

'I'm not so sure,' said Hannah, 'that Lord Byron would have made a good husband for one of my daughters, despite being a member of the nobility.'

'Who would then, Mamma?' asked Emily, cunningly trapping her mother into answering an awkward question.

Hannah was always more prepared for such moments than was her husband and failed to be intimidated by her daughter's queries.

'I'm not so sure, if you were ever to marry, that someone more sensible and down-to-earth, such as

48

a bank manager or a stockbroker might not be the best person to help contain that restless energy of yours.'

'Uggghh, how *boring!*'

'Don't make vulgar noises, dear. A husband doesn't have to be an aristocratic poet to be exciting, my love. He can have quite an ordinary job, like your father, and still be a good and faithful husband.'

'No, but Byron was *exciting*, wasn't he?' said Emily, pirouetting gracefully as she laid the table with cutlery. 'He used to drink wine, write poetry and ride to hounds, all at the same time.'

'Stop spinning round, dear, it makes me dizzy. Did Lord Byron do all that? I can't remember reading about it. I should think it must have been extraordinarily difficult – a circus feat, in fact.'

'Not really. He would have his wine glass in one hand and in the other, a pencil. He would have a note-pad strapped to his right knee – and he used his heels to tell his horse what to do. I think he was a genius. Papa says a genius must be able to do many things? Well, Byron could do them all at once.'

Her mother looked unimpressed. 'And you dreamed all this?'

'No, I *read* about that, in a preface to *Don Juan*. What I dreamed was that he had a hairy chest, like a gorilla. It tickled me.'

Hannah stopped in mid-action at this and stared at her daughter with some concern. With Charlotte their nineteenth-century experiment, or rather as James wished to call it, their *experience*, seemed to be working. Emily however, and possibly Anne, seemed more restless than their eldest daughter. Hannah was beginning to worry for their happiness. It did matter to her whether they would be contented or not, once they reached adulthood. Now here was Emily beginning to reveal the awakenings of sexual feelings.

Emily, partly guessing her mother's thought, said blushingly, 'It's all right, Mother, we were *married*.'

Hannah said, 'Sometimes, child, you horrify me. I suppose we can't be everywhere, in your dreams as well, in order to protect you from yourself, but you do worry me.'

'Yes, Mamma.'

'Now help me cut up this hare your father brought in the other day. It's been hanging long enough, I think.'

'It smells rotten,' said Emily, bluntly.

'Hares need to be hung for a few days, like pheasants, otherwise the meat has a tough taste.'

'Yes, Mamma,' said Emily.

She assisted her mother in removing the skin by slitting the hare down the middle and up to the paw on the underside of the legs, then peeling the pelt away from the flesh. Then the headless, bare carcass was gutted. The meat was put inside a jug which was itself to be placed in a saucepan of water and boiled until the jugged hare was ready.

The pair then continued with the breakfast preparations in silence, until they heard some more stirrings from above, and someone descended the staircase to the lower floor.

'On a point of natural science,' said Hannah, just before anyone else came into the kitchen, 'gorillas do not have hair on their chests. They have it most other places on their bodies, but not on their chests.'

'Yes, Mamma,' whispered Emily.

'Now,' said her mamma, 'would you please go down to the cellar and fetch me some of the special potatoes. Your father likes fried potatoes with his bacon.'

Emily turned pale. 'Oh, Mamma, not the cellar – *please*.'

Hannah turned and stared at her daughter.

'Sometimes,' she said, 'you are the most foolish of children.'

'It frightens me, Mamma. You know it does. I *won't* go down there. I won't.'

'Won't is not a word of which your father approves.'

Nevertheless, Emily stood her ground. It would have taken more than the threat of her father to make her enter the cellar. In the end Hannah had to go herself.

After breakfast, Emily escaped from the house. There was an unspoken rule that the girls did *not* go out of the house alone, but Anne was feeling unwell and had remained in bed, and Charlotte was looking after her. Charlotte disliked being round a sick bed, especially Anne's, but was always the first to offer assistance. Emily knew this was because Charlotte felt it her duty to suffer for her sister's sake. Emily believed Charlotte was doing penance for some imagined sin, like some nun with a tortured soul, desperate for atonement.

Emily had recently asked Charlotte if she thought she could ever fall in love.

Charlotte had replied, 'Love is too fine a thing for a dark spirit such as mine, Em.'

'Silly!' Emily had told her sister. 'There's nothing wrong with your spirit, Charlotte. It's as pure as fresh snow. It's all in your imagination.'

'I don't think I could make a man happy, Emily. Papa told me so, once. He said I was too withdrawn – too distant. I'm inclined to think he was right. I'm much too fond of my own company and my thoughts are sometimes strange. I like the brooding marshes and the wild seabirds. I like dark nights and small rooms. I'm much too strange to fall in love with.'

'You're much too good, that's what you are,' Emily had stated.

Emily found Dan laying a hawthorn hedge. He was cutting live branches 'as thick as a lamb's tongue' partway through, and weaving them between the thicker stems. It was skilful work, Emily could see that, and Dan carried it out with the careful eye and hands of an artist. All the while he worked, he moaned about the cold, and how much easier fences were to maintain than hedges. It *was* bitterly cold, the wind blowing from the east – 'direct from Siberia,' Dan said – and she could see his thick-skinned, calloused hands were red and raw.

'Shouldn't you be wearing gloves?' asked Emily, her hands deep in her warm mittens.

'Can't work with *gloves* on,' grumbled Dan. 'Got to have the touch to make it acc'rate.'

Looking along the line of the hedge, Emily could see how uniform were its patterns, as it lay like a dark, loosely woven scarf over the flatlands. The hedge actually separated the marshes from the pasture land in the centre of the island, so that the cattle would not wander into the bog and get trapped in deep mud. On one side of the hedge was grass and on the other, a little way back, red fescue, sea milkwort and buck's-thorn plantain. In the distance was the River Roach, beyond which stood the village of Paglesham, a place Emily had never visited.

'You goin' to stand there starin' all day, or are you goin' to help me with this?' grumbled Dan.

'What shall I do?' asked Emily, aware she would not have a great deal of time before someone came looking for her.

'You can hold these 'ere twigs back, while I cuts the secondaries.'

Emily did so, as always delighting in outdoor work, which brought her closer to the outside world. The adventurer in her wanted to be strolling along the distant dykes. The little girl in her held her firmly to her home base. There would come a day when the adventurer would triumph and the little girl would be left behind to watch her older self walk from the island.

At one time she saw herself spending the whole of her life on Rattan Island, never needing to leave. But a feeling of being trapped, imprisoned, was growing within her day by day now. Now she wanted to look forward to a time when she would be free to come and go as and when she pleased. Her world on Rattan Island had shrunk since her infant years, to a place quite small and suffocating. There was a wider world waiting for her on the other side of the creek.

5

It was Saturday morning and England was in the icy-fingered grasp of an intense cold spell. Breath froze into fern patterns on windows. Hands and feet were like iron-heavy weights on the ends of unfeeling limbs. Glasses of water were freezing solid on bedside tables overnight. Old people were dying of hypothermia and birds were dying of thirst. Foxes, on the edge of hunger madness, were entering kitchens through cat doors and raiding waste bins.

According to the news the sea had frozen over around the coast of East Anglia. Lakes and pools in and around Paglesham were being used as skating rinks by the local people. Chris had decided it was time to attempt his expedition to Rattan Island. He could always come back, he told himself, if he found himself getting into trouble. The marshes and creeks were not so dangerous when iced over. Such winters as this made accessible places which were normally impossible to reach.

The cold air bit into his nose and cheeks with sharp teeth.

On his way along the snaking earthen wall however, he suddenly came across a youth, sitting on the cold concrete roof of a World War II pill-box. The dykes facing the sea were studded with these ugly antiquities, buried into the side of the earth and turf, used now as toilets by fishermen caught short. By the time Chris realised the muffled youth was in fact Jason Swan, it was too late to go back without looking as if he was running away, though he would liked to have done so.

Two fishing rods lay by Swan's side and the youth appeared intent on playing with a Game Boy. Swan was wrapped up well in thick anorak, scarf, woollen hat and waders. Chris's heart sank as the class bully looked up to see him there. Swan stared hard, making Chris quake inside. Swan not only ruled the playground, he ruled the whole of Chris's world. It was best to avoid tyrants whenever possible, but once in the presence of a despot, you simply waited and hoped he was in good humour.

Today, it seemed, Swan was in a good mood.

'Wuppa, Hatchly,' Swan growled, in the local greeting. 'Where're you going?'

'Just walking,' said Chris, guardedly. 'You fishing?'

'Looks like it, don't it?' Swan said, sarcastically. 'Me old man's gone off to the Plough and Sail for a pint, then we're going home.'

Chris could see what he meant. The tide was out, leaving a thin trickle of fresh water in the centre of the broad tidal river, not more than two metres wide, and this was frozen into a silver snail-like trail in the middle of the mud.

Chris went to pass Swan, who stuck out a leg to stop him.

'Got any fags?' he asked.

'No,' Chris replied.

'Dope?'

Chris wasn't sure whether he was being asked if he had any drugs on him or was being called a name. He had no direct knowledge of the drug scene and didn't want any. Rumours went round the school but he was inclined to think that most of it was just talk: older boys showing off.

Chris shrugged a no.

'Not much good to me then, are you?' said Swan.

The leg was lowered and Swan continued playing with his Game Boy, seemingly oblivious of Chris's presence.

Chris carried on walking around the dyke, a little heartened by the encounter. It had been uncomfortable, but Swan had not seemed unduly hostile. Perhaps he was softening? Nevertheless, Chris didn't feel like passing him on the way back, when the other boy's whole attitude might have altered.

The sky was a cold slab of marble. A knife-edged wind was coming from across the river. Even the wading birds were silent. Farmland stretched out beyond the dyke, fields like sheets of corrugated steel. Trees, singly or in small groups, stood stark and black against the still, troubled heavens. Lumpy pastures were empty of domestic animals.

Chris found the place where the river was at its narrowest and crossing would be easier than elsewhere. Rattan Island lay on the other side. He descended the dyke and went out on to mud which would normally have sucked him down to his thighs. Now it was as hard as cooled volcanic lava. Slipping a little in his boots, he went down the quarter-mile of gentle slope to the sliver of ice where was the low-water river in the centre. Then up again to the dyke on the other side.

Triumphant, he stood on the top and, seeing the figure of Swan on the far bank, he instinctively waved.

Swan did not return the gesture. Embarrassed, Chris jumped down from the top of the dyke, to the ditch below. Crossing this, he began stepping out over the frozen ground of the misty salt marsh which ringed Rattan Island. He knew that with a farm on the island he would have to keep a wary eye open for dogs. It was the most exciting adventure he had ever undertaken, especially as he had to pass one or two of those notices which warned him that he was trespassing on private land.

His journey eventually took him to an unclimbable hedge, which he followed until he reached a wire fence. Slipping between the wires of the fence, and then through some curtains of crack willow, he found himself at the back of a large, two-storey house. A chest-high wooden fence, surrounding a small lawn, separated him from the dwelling. So long as he stayed on the right side of that fence, he felt he was not *really* trespassing, though he knew the whole of Rattan Island belonged to the owner of this austere-looking dwelling.

He stared at the main window of the farmhouse, seeing figures in the room beyond. Instinctively, he ducked down, only to peer over the top when no one came out. Probably because the day was dull they had switched on the room light. Chris could see three girls, of varying ages. One of the girls, the tallest and slimmest of the three, was to his eyes quite beautiful. He had seen her before, through his father's binoculars.

He continued to stare at the extraordinary sight.

For some reason the girls were dressed as maids and he guessed there was a game in progress. Certainly they were laughing.

He watched for ages, observing the three girls, feeling strange knowing that he was spying on their games without their knowledge. It felt wrong, in a sense, yet it was wonderfully pleasurable. Too pleasurable to resist, despite the risk of being discovered. He knew his mother would have disapproved of him peering into a private house, at three young women. He also felt guilty of invading their home, even though he was not inside. But he couldn't turn away.

The skin on his face tingled as he watched one of them stand up and twirl, her long grey skirts billowing. He felt like some Greek god, standing in the shadows of the trees on the edge of a sunlit glade in which nymphs and dryads frolicked unaware.

Then something, some movement on his part, must have attracted their attention. One of them looked out of the window, pointed, and the other two stared. He was trapped, caught peeping, and he felt hot blood rush to his face.

The girls continued looking at him, with astonished expressions. He might have been an elephant, wandered away from the zoo, going by their faces. The tableau remained frozen for a while, then one of them stepped forward and gave him a little smile and a wave. He gulped in confusion. The other two came forward now, still wide-eyed with apparent surprise.

Chris suddenly caught a movement in the corner of his eye, over by one of the barns, and he gave the three girls a quick wave and a smile, then ducked through the willows.

He hurriedly retraced his steps, climbing over the fence back into the marshes, which he crossed at a run. Had the weather been normal, he would probably have fallen into a bog and drowned. Once he reached the river basin he saw that there was actually a tide coming in, though not as fast and as full as usual, and he quickly crossed the frozen mud to the middle, where he managed to get his feet wet fording the brackish water.

Once on his own shore, and safe, he walked slowly back along the dyke to Paglesham. Thankfully, Swan was no longer perched on the pill-box, and Chris did not have to worry about whether to greet Swan as a friend, or ignore him, either of which might have proved the wrong approach.

When Chris arrived home, he saw that Tom's car was parked outside.

Chris did not especially *like* Tom, as his father probably imagined he did, but he knew that Tom was company for his mother. So, in that respect, Chris was pleased to see him at the house occasionally. Sally was still not convinced that she ought to be seeing another man, but Tom was one of those people who kept turning up anyway, on some pretext or another, even though she had told him she wanted no more 'dates' for a while.

Chris took off his boots at the door then opened it and stepped inside in his wet socks. He hoped his mother would not notice, but she was sitting in the chair by the fire, across from the doorway.

'What *have* you been doing?' she asked, sitting up.

'Don't fuss, Mum. I've just been down to the river and the water went over the top of my boots.'

'*In the river?*'

'Not in it. The tide was out. It was only a couple of ticks ago anyway. My feet haven't been wet for long. I'll go and get some more socks on.'

Tom Garfield was sitting in the other chair, drinking a mug of tea or coffee. He was a lean, almost cadaverous-looking man, with short, cropped hair. Untidy and a little unkempt, he was nothing like Chris's father. Jack Hatchly was a smart, handsome man-about-town, while Tom Garfield was a fairly ordinary man-around-somewhere. Jack always seemed at his ease in any old or new situation, while Tom always looked out of place, wherever he happened to be.

'You have to treat the river with a bit of respect,' said Tom. 'These tidal estuary rivers are pretty dangerous.'

'I know that,' retorted Chris, with some irritability.

'Yes, I'm sure you do,' smiled the unruffled Tom.

Chris went upstairs to his room, took off his wet socks and wiped his feet with a towel, then put on some clean socks from the chest of drawers in his own room.

Chris did not want to go downstairs and make small talk, so he stayed in his room, lying on his bed. He thought about the three girls he had seen at the farm. They had all been dark-haired and pretty. He liked the tall, very pretty girl, with the beautiful eyes. He tried to remember if she was the one who had waved to him, but he had been in such a state of embarrassment at the time his memory failed him.

The tall one though! She had been really something. Better-looking than Swan's girlfriend, Tanya. Weird clothes though: a bit dowdy. Swan's girl was a Goth who dressed all in black, with black lace gloves, black spiky hair and dark lipstick on her peaky, pale face. Chris was willing to admit to everyone but Swan that he found Tanya exciting. Goths were something wild, poetic and strange.

This girl in the house though, she'd looked like some sort of Cinderella. And her sisters too. They'd all been dressed in the same kind of stuff, with aprons and funny little maids' caps on their heads. Maybe they'd just been playing a game, but they looked a bit old for that. Unless, he suddenly thought, unless they were practising for some sort of school play? Perhaps a kind of Florence Nightingale thing?

He liked girls who were confident enough to go on the stage, since he himself would have shrivelled and died before stepping out under the footlights. He just *had* to see her again. He *had* to. Maybe if he could find out which school she went to, he could meet her afterwards? They could go to see a film, or ten-pin bowling on the pier, or whatever appealed to her? Chris had all sorts of romantic ideas.

His mother suddenly appeared in the doorway holding up his wet boots.

'What am I supposed to do with these, young man?' she said.

He rose, sheepishly. 'I'll put them in the bathroom to dry by the radiator.'

'See that you do.' She placed them on the floor, near to the doorway. She then went to her own bedroom.

Chris did as he was told, then went downstairs. Tom was still in the living-room, but standing admiring the view from the window. He turned slightly on hearing Chris and nodded.

'Wish I lived out here in the country,' he said. 'It's so peaceful.'

Chris shrugged. 'You wouldn't say that if the pigeons woke you every morning.'

'Ah, but the sound of the birds – the dawn chorus – that's pleasant compared with traffic.'

'Pigeons make a *boring* noise – coo, coo, coo, coo – hours on end. It drives you crazy. If I was allowed an airgun I'd shoot them.'

Chris liked to shock Tom, when he could.

'I can't imagine you'd do that,' said Tom. 'Last time I spoke to you, you were telling me off for all the pollution in the world and you said you would vote Green once you were old enough.'

'Rats and cockroaches and things are all right,' said Chris, 'but I'd shoot pigeons and feed 'em to the foxes.'

'Would you now?' said Tom, realising at last that he was being kidded. 'What else would you kill?'

'Oh, harmless ring-doves, songbirds, stray puppies – give 'em to the weasels and stoats, I say.'

Chris went into the kitchen and got himself a lemonade, before returning to the living-room. Tom was sitting down again, looking into the fire. He seemed a little out of sorts.

'Are you going out tonight?' asked Chris, sipping his drink.

'What?' Tom looked up sharply. 'Oh, no. Your mum doesn't think it's a good idea.'

'I do. I think you should ask her again.'

'Do you? I'm inclined to think it wouldn't be any good. She's pretty adamant about not going on another date with me.'

'She'll change her mind,' said Chris. 'You wait and see. She's still mooning after Dad.'

'I'd like to think she would come out with me again,' Tom said, with some hope in his voice. 'That is,' he added, 'if I thought you would get your father back, I'd disappear, obviously. A boy needs his father . . .'

'Not me,' said Chris, resolutely. 'I don't want him. He can go to – well, I just don't want him back, that's all.'

6

Emily was in Charlotte's bedroom. It was mid-afternoon.

Father had gone on one of his twice-weekly trips to the mainland post office to collect the mail.

Mother was feeling melancholy and had locked herself in the downstairs bathroom. The girls knew she would be in there for at least an hour, perhaps two. Over the last two or three years they had come to accept that their mother suffered sad thoughts sometimes, weeping for reasons of her own. Emily thought it was over an early lover, someone before her father: a man who had gone away to war or sea and never returned. Charlotte believed her mother was unhappy because of her father, though she was not able to discover why.

James Craster was unaware of his wife's habit and the girls never spoke of it to anyone but each other and their observations were confined to simply reporting to each other that mother was 'unavailable'. It was one of their dark secrets.

Anne was not feeling well and was lying on the living-room sofa, in front of a roaring fire, with a blanket over her and one or two reading books within reach.

Charlotte was reading to Emily from *Idylls of the King*.

'In Love, if Love be Love, if Love be ours,
Faith and unfaith can ne'er be equal powers:
Unfaith is aught . . .'

Emily interrupted with, 'Can you keep a secret?'

Charlotte looked up from her book and said, 'You know I can, dearest Em.'

Emily's voice fell to a whisper. 'I feel an affection for that boy who looked into our window. He's so – so *handsome*, Charlotte. Don't you think so? I think he likes *me*, too – I noticed him staring at me. His hair looked so beautiful. I wanted to touch his face. Will he come back, do you think? I dream about him every night.'

Charlotte's eyes widened. 'Em, how could you? You don't know anything about him. He's probably some common boy from the town. You might hate him as soon as he opens his mouth to speak. You know what Father says about young men – they're dreadfully selfish creatures. Look what happened to the maid of Neidpath, when her lover knight returned: "He came – he pass'd – an heedless gaze, as o'er some stranger glancing." It broke her heart that he didn't even recognise her, after she'd waited for him all those years.'

'I dreamed about him last night,' said Emily, fiercely. 'I *like* him. *Mon coeur bat très vite avec l'amour.*'

The word that it was not possible to say in English could be thinly disguised by using French.

'But what do you *know* about it all, Em?' pleaded Charlotte.

Emily looked her sister in the eyes and smiled.

Charlotte was asking Emily what she knew about

65

love and affection and Charlotte knew the answer herself. Emily knew *all* about love: as much as any human being would ever know about it. Charlotte, Emily and even Anne had been spoon-fed poetry about love for all of their short lives. They had read and been read Burns, Keats, Shelley, Byron, Scott, Browning, Colonel Lovelace, Marvell, Donne and many, many others. Some had been censored by their father, who didn't approve of certain poems, such as Marvell's 'To His Coy Mistress', but for the most part the girls had read widely and deeply on the subject of love, by those who professed to come closest to explaining just what it was and what it was all about – the poets.

It was no good telling Emily that, because she had never seen a boy before and therefore had never been in love, she could not understand what it meant. Her argument against this, in her own words, was that people in love are the last to understand it. People in love, Emily informed her sister, are so blinded by the intensity of the feeling, so overcome by the flood-tide of emotions, they have not the least understanding of it. Understanding came only by taking a step back, studying with the impartial eyes of the observer.

'I know all about love, Charlotte dear, and so do you – we've read every book ever written on the subject.'

'Well,' said Charlotte, 'we shan't see the boy again, so I suppose there's no harm in dreaming.'

Emily said nothing, for in her heart she knew the young man would be back again. He had looked into her eyes and a flame had sprung up between them. He would brave the marshes, the weather, and her papa's wrath, simply to catch a glimpse of her beauty. He had been smitten by the same spell which had overcome *her*.

At five o'clock, Papa returned with the letters and parcels. Mamma had emerged from the bathroom by that time. The girls descended the stairs, greeting their father as if he had been on a long journey and had not seen Haworth Farm for a year. Even Anne rose from her sickbed on the sofa to kiss her father's cheek and tell him how happy she was to see him home safely. There was always quiet drama in the house, to stimulate the girls' imaginations and emotions.

And now there was much excitement.

Some of the parcels contained books, purchased from a mail-order firm which specialised in obtaining works that were out of print. There were books on art, poetry, music. There were critical works on literature. There were novels. None of the books had a publication date later than 1900. It might have been Christmas in the Craster household, as the girls unwrapped the stained and musty-smelling books and exclaimed over them in delight.

After the excitement was over, James Craster went out to see how Dan Selby had got on during his absence.

Dan was herding the milking cows into their stalls.

'What's going on, Selby?' said James Craster in an abrupt tone. 'What's happened here?'

'Nothin' untoward,' said Dan Selby, well-used to his boss's lack of friendliness.

However polite and gentlemanly James Craster was to his wife and daughters, he was regarded by any workers with whom he came into contact as a bit of a foul-mouthed tyrant. Out of earshot of his family he could let rip with the choicest language, had a temper like a storm at sea, and would even threaten those who displeased him with physical violence. Dan had put up with him for years because James Craster paid him well, mainly to keep his mouth shut about what went on at Haworth Farm.

'Why are you so late in bringing in the cows? It's been dark for an hour.'

Dan looked his employer in the eyes. 'I thought we might have a prowler – I found some footprints.'

James Craster frowned. 'What do you mean, footprints?'

'Can't say I knows how to put it any other way in English,' said Dan, a little sarcastically. 'Footprints is footprints. Get yourself a torch an' I'll show you.'

James Craster went to the tack shed and found a torch, while Dan put the cows to bed. Then the pair of them went to the marsh behind the hawthorn hedge. There, framed by a circular cowpat, was the sunken mark of a booted foot. It belonged neither to Dan nor to James Craster himself, and in the winter there were no other workers on the farm. It was obvious to James Craster that someone had been stalking around the farmhouse, possibly looking for something to steal.

Because of the soft nature of the dung it was impossible to tell how large the man had been.

'I take it you haven't *seen* anyone?' he asked Dan.

'If I had I wouldn't be botherin' to show you these 'ere footprints – I'd tell you about him.'

James Craster nodded, the fury rising in him. How *dare* someone trespass on his land! How *dare* they! No doubt the intruder had sneaked in during the night. Well, he would soon put a stop to such activities. They would know who they were dealing with if they came again.

'Lay some steel gin traps,' snapped James Craster. 'There's several in the tack shed, under some sacking. I can always say I put them down for foxes, if we get any trouble.'

'They're not legal,' Dan argued, stony-faced. 'You could break a man's leg with one o' them.'

'I don't give a damn whether they're a hanging offence, I want them laid along this hedge.'

Dan said, 'An' what happens if a cow treads on one – or one of your own daughters?'

James Craster stared thoughtfully at his man. 'My daughters don't go on to the marsh.'

'What happens if you has a fire and they all comes runnin' out of the house in a panic? What happens if one gets tearful for some'at and runs off without thinkin'? What are you going to tell their mother when them pretty little anklebones gets crushed in these man traps, eh? I'm not tellin' you you can't do it – I'm just arskin' you to think of the possible consequences of an accident. You'd not forgive me, nor yourself.'

Dan Selby's reason prevailed. Now that the initial wave of fury had passed hotly through James Craster, he began to think more rationally. It was true that gin traps were dangerous things to have close to a house. He would have to think about it further. In the meantime he needed to protect his family.

'Before you come to work tomorrow, Selby, call

in at Marchant's and pick up some security lights – those that come on when an intruder is around. I know the animals will set them off, but I want them anyway. We'll run them from the generator.'

'Right, Mr Craster – lights. I'll get some tomorrow.'

'And I don't want Mrs Craster or the girls to know we've had a prowler, you understand? It might worry them.'

'Right.'

The two men went back to the farmhouse, where Selby said goodnight and set out on his bicycle along the cockleshell track which led across the marshes to Rattan Hard, which forded Rattan Creek in the south. Dan lived in the village of Barling, just beyond the creek.

A stranger could, of course, have come over the hard and used the selfsame track to reach Haworth Farm, but there were notices all the way along, threatening trespassers with a fate just short of death. James Craster had always found these notices, and the various gates wrapped in barbed wire, to be effective deterrents to walkers venturing where they were not welcome.

Even if thieves knew of the existence of the farm, the area was bleak and forbidding, and there was no reason why they would want to run the risk of the marshes or the hard, to reach a farmhouse which might have little to offer in the way of easy-to-carry loot, when there were much easier and more accessible houses to rob elsewhere.

The cockleshell track was not solid enough to support a vehicle bigger than the pony and trap, which James Craster used to visit the mainland, so no cars or lorries could get to the farmhouse. Shire horses were used for the heavy work around the farm: two big uncomplaining mares. There was no tractor, no farmer's road vehicle. Any new livestock purchased was driven across the hard by a man on foot and up the long straight cockleshell track to the farm. Piglets or heifers were strapped on to a cart and the pony was used to transport them.

The farmhouse then was only vulnerable to the thief who was either stupid or insane enough to run stupid risks.

That evening James Craster took a twelve-bore double-barrelled shotgun from a gun cupboard in his study and loaded it with cartridges. To keep a loaded weapon in the house was illegal but he cared little for legalities he knew he could flout. He left the safety catch on, but locked the gun securely away again since one of his daughters had once got hold of it.

It had been at a time when Charlotte had been in a depressed state of mind and had tried, in a number of ways, to hurt herself. Although she had been warned to expect periods by her mother, who told all the girls that they were women's punishment for the sin of Eve, she hated them. They made her feel dirty and totally undignified, not the least because they left her feeling drained and weak. It was during a heavy period that Charlotte became morose and withdrawn. She had somehow managed to get hold of the shotgun and James Craster was sure would have hurt herself with it if he had not discovered her in time.

This was one of the darker secrets that lived in the house, never mentioned by anyone, but which remained lurking amongst the rafters, in dark corners, waiting for a release which might never come. It was like the large ship rat in their cellar which could not be caught: silently acknowledged by all, but never spoken of openly.

Later, James Craster went out again to the hawthorn hedge and stared over the marshes. He could see nothing but the lights of Paglesham to the west and the lights of Barling to the south. That was as it should be. Normally there were boats drifting along the river at high tide, their lights visible from the house, but not since the cold spell had arrived.

'You come here again, mister,' said James Craster under his breath, 'and I'll blow your head off for you.'

7

Monday was a bad day for Chris.

When he got up that morning, his mother told him his father wanted to meet him after school.

'What for?' asked Chris, irritably.

'Well,' Sally said, 'he *is* your father. You must see him from time to time. He's entitled to that much.'

'When I'm eighteen,' Chris vowed, darkly. 'I won't have to meet *anyone* I don't want to.'

Sally smiled. 'If that includes me, young man, you're going to have a tough time. I know you help me quite a lot around the house now, but that isn't half of it, Chrissie . . .'

He *hated* being called Chrissie and went up to his room to sulk until it was time for school. Once he arrived at school, the day got no better. Swan met him in the crowded playground.

'Was that you muckin' about over the other side of the river, Hatchface? You was trespassing, wasn't you? You could go inside for that – you could get banged up.'

Chris knew this was a lie, but he didn't say so.

'So what?' he said at last.

'So *what*? You tryin' to be the big hero, Hatchly? Leave it out. What was that poncey stuff with the hand?'

'I only waved.'

'Waved? Waaaaved?' he sniggered for the benefit of the watchers. 'You prat. Waved, didja?'

Onlookers laughed and jeered, as Swan flipped a limp-wristed hand in his face.

The anger washed through Chris like a flood. For once he allowed his feelings to get the better of him. With a hot face he snapped, 'Don't call me names, Swan.'

That quietened the crowd, to a deathly silence, as Swan's face turned to stone. He moved up close to Chris, nose to nose, standing about a centimetre away. Chris could smell the sour odour of Marmite and toast on his enemy's breath. He wanted to back up but Tilvey, one of Swan's cronies, was standing on his heels.

Swan said, 'You better take that back, Hatchly.'

Chris jabbed back with his elbow and felt it sink satisfyingly into a soft stomach. Tilvey doubled up with an 'Oooooofff,' and staggered away, leaving Chris room to get out of Swan's way.

'You stay away from me, Duckface,' cried Chris, throwing all caution to the winds. He looked around wildly and, seeing Ishwinder Singh standing nearby, added, 'Me and my mate Ish are fed up of being messed around by you lot. Singh means lion, y'know – Sikhs fight like crazy when they have to.' On seeing Ishwinder's eyes popping, Chris panicked further and elaborated even more recklessly. 'Yeah, Ish has learned karate, see!'

At that moment the bell went for lessons. Chris's temper cooled down and his head became full of wild thoughts. I've really done it now, he thought. Swan wouldn't rest until Chris was once more an abject creature, cringing every time Swan hove into

74

sight. Chris was heading for a beating, as sure as sugar was sweet, and he'd probably take Ishwinder with him.

'Thanks a lot,' hissed Ishwinder angrily, showing his gratitude for Chris's involvement of him in the crisis. 'I really appreciate that. I'll remember you in my will.'

So, it was a miserable Chris, who went into David Gates's maths class and suddenly realised he had not done the homework set on Friday. When asked for it, Chris said to David Gates, 'Can I bring it tomorrow?'

'Haven't you finished it? There wasn't a great deal.'

'I – I didn't get time.'

'Got time to muck about over the river,' muttered Swan, from the other side of the classroom.

'That'll do, Swan,' said David Gates. 'I'm quite capable of dealing with this myself. Hatchly, you'll do exercise 27, as well as 26, as a punishment. Any arguments?'

'No,' said Chris, wanting to burst into tears, or yell and scream, or smash a desk to pieces – anything to relieve the enormous frustration that threatened him with bursting.

Somehow he got through the day, managing to avoid retribution from Swan by going into the library at lunchtime. Ishwinder was not so lucky, but told Chris he had to deny any friendship between them, several times, before he was allowed to go on his way unharmed. Ishwinder knew, as did Chris really, that there was no escaping Swan.

Swan was tough *and* intelligent, a rare combination, and it was hard to defeat such a boy in anything. Academic teachers put up with his behaviour because he got good grades. Games teachers liked him because he was physically superior to most boys. He represented the school at swimming and diving, which caused them to overlook his hostility and aggressive behaviour. It was wrongly believed that boys like Swan were superior at sport *because* they had a touch of the barbarian in them.

Swan was the king because most teachers allowed him extra licence and turned a blind eye to bad conduct.

After school was over, Chris hurried out, crossed the playground and walked to the waiting line of cars, looking for his mother's. However, Swan caught up with him and grabbed him by the shirtfront, seemingly oblivious of all the other parents waiting for their children.

'*Now*, Hatchly . . .'

A man roughly interceded, pulling the boys apart. 'What the hell's going on here?'

It was Chris's father. Chris had forgotten he was being met by Jack. His dad, a head taller than Swan, glowered down on the boy through his black horn-rimmed glasses.

'Mind your own business,' snapped Swan, unabashed.

'Mind my own . . .?' Jack's eyes widened at this insolence and Chris could sense the anger bubbling up inside his father. 'You little squirt. I ought to wring your neck for you.' Jack turned to Chris. 'Who is this nasty little creep? What's his father's name?'

'You don't want to know – my dad would knock

your head off,' Swan said, and whirled away, calling back over his shoulder, 'Remember, Hatchface, *I* rule the playground. I'll see you tomorrow.'

Jack snarled. 'Who is that boy?'

Chris sighed. 'Never mind, Dad. What do you want? Why've you met me from school?'

'Aren't you just a little bit grateful I saved you from a thumping there? I hope you would have stood up for yourself against that vicious little thug.'

'Dad – get real. Swan isn't *little* and he can make mincemeat of me. We've had punch-ups before and they always end the same way. Let's face it, he could give you a run for your money, and he's just coming up sixteen. He doesn't *care* what happens to him. Nobody can beat someone who doesn't care about being hurt. We had a kid called Phillips who was two years ahead of Swan and Swan flattened him in a boxing match, even though Swan had a broken nose.

'There was another boy – a prefect. He tried to tell Swan what to do and Swan knocked him off his bike and kicked in the spokes. A cop came to the school but the teacher stuck up for Swan and said it was an accident . . .'

'That's monstrous!' cried Jack.

'Well, it happens sometimes, Dad. Any other kid would've been expelled, but Swan gets away with it.'

Jack changed the subject. 'You want to go for a Big Mac?'

They went to the fast-food hall in Southend, where Jack lavished money and attention on his son, trying to make up in half an hour for years of negligence. Chris knew this sentimental, remorseful side of his father and he didn't like it any more than the neglectful side. Jack gushed and promised impossible futures, where the two of them would go for a fortnight's trekking and camping in Derbyshire together, or hunting and fishing in Scotland, while Chris knew that even if Jack managed to spend a whole weekend with him on an activity of Chris's choice, here in Essex, it would be a miracle.

The trouble was his father really believed himself, when he painted these scenarios of the two of them.

'When?' asked Chris, sipping his coke, knowing this would stem the tide of promises.

'When?' Jack wrinkled his brow. 'I'll have to look at my calendar. I'll give you a call. If we went to Scotland, we could take Silvia with us – you know I'm seeing someone, a woman called Silvia? I think it's only fair, since your mother's going out with what's-his-name . . .'

'Tom – his name's Tom. And you were seeing Silvia long before Mum met Tom.'

'Yes, well, that's beside the point. Thing is though, I'm pretty booked up for the next six weeks – anyway it's too cold at the moment to go traipsing over the country. Maybe in the summer, when it's warmer . . .

Yeah, yeah, yeah.

Chris was taken home and dropped outside the house. Jack did not try to see Sally. When he did visit it was always when he was least expected, so that the encounter was on his terms, not on anyone else's. He never liked being at a disadvantage in their confrontations.

Chris didn't do his homework, as he had promised David Gates, but went to bed in a foul mood, promising himself he would bunk off school the next day. It would be the first time Chris had failed to turn up for school. He and Ishwinder had a longstanding agreement between them that Chris could use Ishwinder's bike to bunk off whenever he wished, provided he got it back to school in time for Ishwinder to ride home in the evening.

Before he went to bed, Chris went to a drawer which held information on the National Trust, English Heritage and the Ramblers' Association. The drawer also contained Ordnance Survey maps and he took out the one entitled Burnham-on-Crouch Sheet TQ 89/99 1:25000. This was the map which included Rattan Island.

The next day, after Sally dropped him off outside the school. Chris ran to the corner and down a sidestreet. Ten minutes later, Ishwinder came along and, on being requested to do so, handed over his bicycle.

'You're mad, Chris. You're in enough trouble already.'

'Can't get much worse,' said Chris grimly. 'Thanks Ishwinder – you want my sandwiches?'

'Yeah, course.'

The sandwiches were handed over and Chris put his arms through the handles of his sports bag, so that he could wear it on his back like a haversack, and set off for Barling. He was going to visit the farm in the middle of Rattan Island, where he had seen the girls. This time though, he intended going in by the official route, over Rattan Hard.

It was a cold ride to Barling, the weather having improved little since the mini ice age had arrived.

Chris had on only a thin anorak over his school uniform and he was shivering even before he got to the open flatlands beyond the houses. There it was bitter. There was no wind but the coldnesses of the land and sky were like two weights pressing on each other, squeezing the energy out of all living things. There were Brent geese, winter visitors in their thousands, out in the fields near the creeks, pecking away at the iron-hard earth. They were probably wondering why they had ever left their northern climes to journey to this place which was supposed to be warmer.

Chris travelled the road between the creeks, where the water had gouged out great troughs broken only by the occasional island knoll of sea lavender. A maze of waterways crazed the landscapes thereabouts, until he reached Rattan Creek and the hard. There he abandoned Ishwinder's bicycle, chaining it to an iron gate, before climbing the gate and crossing the frozen waterway.

On the island side he found a track strewn with crushed cockleshells, which he guessed led to the house in the centre of Rattan. He followed the track, his shoulders hunched and his hands buried deep in his anorak pockets. Here there were only gulls and the odd crow, the geese preferring to be on arable land or mudflats, rather than on cattle pastures. Notices told him that as a trespasser he would be wise to turn back, but he felt he had a good excuse for being there.

When the large house came into view he slowed down and began to drag his feet. His heart was beating faster now. The dwelling stood on a low rise which left it stark against the light-grey sky, and it looked almost as if it were perched on the edge of the world. It looked formidable, like an ancient keep.

His intention on coming to the farm was to ask if they had any weekend work available for a schoolboy such as him. It was not that he needed money, but he was attracted to the girls he had seen, especially the tall one with the black hair. He wanted to see her again, perhaps get to talk to her. She seemed almost untouchable to him – they all did – but he wanted to get to know her better, perhaps ask her to go out with him.

Once again he was wary of dogs, but this farm, unlike any other he had known, did not seem to own one.

The front of the house, decorated with a little protective porch, had a dark green door. When he stood on the frayed, sodden coconut mat, he saw that there was no bell and no knocker. There were two thin panels of green glass in the door and he rapped on one of these with his knuckles, rattling the pane. The sound seemed to fall dull and leaden on his ears and he wondered if anyone would hear it.

Soon enough, however, he caught sight of a shadow behind the green glass and someone turned the knob and began tugging at the door. It seemed stuck, probably with the damp, so Chris gave it a nudge with his shoulder.

The door suddenly shot open with a rattle and shake, and a young girl of about ten or eleven years of age confronted him. She was dressed in those peculiar clothes he had seen all three of them wearing the last time he had been at the house. Her face looked pale and pinched under the cotton cap.

'Er, hello – I – er, is your dad there?' asked Chris.

'Dad?' asked the girl. Then with clear diction and quaint lilt, she added, 'Oh, you mean Papa? He's out at the north field with Daniel Selby.'

'What about your – your mother? I want to ask about getting some work, you see. Part time – weekend. I don't mind what I do – muck out the stables, whatever.'

'Mamma is unavailable. You're the boy who looked in our window the other day, aren't you? I was feeling quite well then, but not today. I have a mysterious ailment, you see. No one can discover what is the matter with me.'

'Er, yeah,' mumbled Chris, wondering whether someone was playing games with him. 'Your mum's not in then?'

'I told you, Mamma is unavailable. She just went into the bathroom, so she won't be out for quite some time yet.'

'OK, thanks . . .'

He hurried away quickly, wondering what sort of household would leave a batty girl to answer the door. She was definitely weird. Perhaps it was a home for the mentally ill or something?

He heard footsteps running on the cockleshells behind him and he turned to see the second girl. She stopped about two metres from him, her eyes shining. Dressed like her sister, she was not armed against the cold, but she did not seem to mind and was certainly not shivering as much as himself. She stood there, a triumphant look on her face, regarding him.

82

'My name is Emily,' she said at last, 'after Emily Brontë. My sisters are also named after the Brontës – you've met Anne, who is of course the youngest, and Charlotte is the eldest. We have no Branwell, thank goodness, for Papa thinks fickle young men bring a family to ruin. Oh, I do beg your pardon. Those are not my views, of course, and I'm sure you're not fickle.'

Chris was astonished, both at the content of the speech and the manner in which it was delivered. He was dumbfounded, not knowing how to answer. Was she acting? Putting on a voice? Was he the brunt of some elaborate joke? Perhaps there were people in the house, giggling behind the curtains? He shot a quick look at the farm, but could see no evidence that this was a trick. The girl seemed deadly serious. He continued staring at her, wondering what to say in answer.

'Oh, I knew you'd come,' she said, clapping her hands together. 'I just knew it. Did you come to ask me out for a walk? That's very foolish, you know. Papa disapproves of boys and he would be very angry if he knew we were speaking to one another. But I think you're quite brave.'

'Angry?' said Chris at last, rather lamely.

'Oh, *yes*,' replied Emily, her brows knitting together. 'Papa is dreadfully against boys. It makes it rather unfortunate for us girls, because we are not permitted to meet them, you see. I'm sure Papa thinks we shall act in a silly fashion, like Lydia in *Pride and Prejudice*. But of course, none of us are silly. We are all quite sensible.' She smiled and added candidly, 'I suppose I'm the *least* sensible.'

Chris felt as if he was dreaming. He was certain

he wasn't being taken for a ride now, but he was unsure how to handle this strange girl who spoke really posh. He had never met an upper-class family, but surely this was the way they would talk? Maybe her father was some kind of gentleman farmer, an aristocrat fallen on hard times? It seemed the most likely explanation.

'What about your sister – the tall one? Charlotte? Isn't she old enough to go out with boys?'

'Oh no. None of us are expected to meet with boys.'

'I'd better go then,' said Chris, imagining a furious farmer bearing down on him with a sharp sickle.

'Please,' she said, taking one neat step nearer to him and standing like a Dutch Doll, feet together. 'Please will you tell me your address, so that I may write you a letter, as a friend? Shall I write to you? I have no one else to write to and I should so like a pen-friend – especially you.'

'If you like,' muttered Chris, warily.

'Well then, where do you live? Tell me. I have an excellent memory – I memorise verses by the dozen.'

A little against his better judgement, he blurted out his address. Then for some reason he found himself holding out his hand and she stepped forward again and shook it briskly. He found her open enthusiasm hard to resist. It was a shame that she wasn't the older one – Charlotte? – but she was quite pretty in her way. Not so slim and elegant, but she seemed to like him well enough. The black curls which had escaped her little cap bobbed as she nodded, her eyes full of the dark lights of eagerness.

'Please don't write back to me here, though. Papa would not like it at all. I shall tell you what you must do.'

'I was going to ask your dad for work.'

Emily shook her head firmly. 'Papa would never give you work. He doesn't like young men.'

Chris nodded and then strode away, anxious to get some ground between himself and the house where 'Papa' lived. He was in enough trouble already and he knew he could not afford to antagonise yet another adult.

Once he was over the hard and cycling along the bare road, he thought again about the dark young woman. Emily was closer to his age than Charlotte, that much was certain. And the skin on her hand had been like silk to the touch. It had melted his stomach. She was so full of life too. Perhaps she might turn out to be the best one of the three?

A magpie strutted out into the road ahead.

'HEY!' yelled Chris, suddenly overcome by excitement. 'Out of the way, bird, out of the way.'

He swished past the affronted magpie, laughing when it hopped into a short flight.

When he finally reached the street by the school, where he was to hand over the bike to his pal, Chris was still feeling buoyant and happy. Something good had happened to him at last. Somebody liked him. A *girl* liked him. A very attractive girl who wore funny clothes and spoke in a peculiar way, but so what? He liked the way she talked. It was different. She was different. It was *great*.

8

'Stay behind after class is over,' said David Gates to Chris.

Heads swung to look at the condemned boy. Swan smiled in his snidey way and nodded.

'And you, Swan. I want to see you, too.'

'What for?' said Swan, suddenly glowering.

'The reason I've asked you, is so that I can tell you,' replied David Gates evenly.

The lesson proceeded. Chris had done all the homework asked of him and handed it in. He expected David Gates to melt a little, but the teacher remained grim and businesslike. He merely nodded curtly and took the exercise book.

When the other pupils had left, Chris and Swan remained at their desks. Swan was fiddling with a pencil, skilfully twirling it around his fingers with one hand. David Gates crooked a finger, motioning both boys to come to him at the front of the class.

The teacher spoke first to Chris. 'Do you have a legitimate excuse for being absent yesterday?'

Chris decided there was no escaping the truth. 'No, sir. I bunked off.'

'In that case, report to Mr Leggitt at lunchtime.' Mr Leggitt was the Housemaster.

'Yes, sir.' Chris turned to go, but David Gates raised a finger to keep him there.

'Wait. I've had a report of a bullying incident. It involved both of you.'

Swan glowered hatred at Chris, but David Gates said, 'You can wipe that look off your face, Swan. It wasn't Hatchly that reported it, it was a parent who saw you in front of the school. It's not the first incident that's come to my notice, but it's the first involving a reliable witness . . .'

Swan was looking bored, staring at the window.

'PAY ATTENTION, BOY!' yelled David Gates, his face dark with anger.

Swan jumped, so did Chris. David Gates was one of those teachers for whom the children had a great deal of unspoken respect. You could joke with him, but you couldn't mess him around. He was not a large man, but he was very tough, and scared of no one. Even Swan, who said he didn't give a damn about adults, was normally careful not to antagonise David Gates.

'You don't have to shout like that,' Swan said. 'I'm not deaf. If you can't tell when a person's mulling something over in his mind . . .'

'Now you listen to me, Swan,' said David Gates through his teeth. 'If I send you to the headmaster, as I should, you'll be expelled instantly.'

Swan looked about to protest, but David Gates's eyes warned him against it.

'*Instantly*. You understand? There's been a big crackdown on bullying in Essex lately and the head's just looking for an example to show the authorities that this school is no different from others. Now, the threat of expulsion may hold little fear for you, Swan – we all know what a hard case you are – but let me tell you what it will entail.

'You won't be allowed back into *this* school, that much you do know. What will happen is that your parents . . .'

'My dad,' Swan corrected. 'You might remember from open day that my mother never comes to the school. She's had a breakdown, so leave her out of it.'

'Right. Your father, with others, will attempt to get you into another school. When they find one, and the holiday's over, it may be at the other end of the country. The school will know why you've been sent there and they'll watch you like hawks. If you foul up again, the whole process will repeat itself. Believe me, Swan, if you think this chat is boring, it'll be nothing to being dragged around from school to school, from head to head, having to make new friends, finding yourself further and further away from home. You won't have time for bullying – you'll be too busy commuting. Finally, when you're old enough – which isn't that far away – you'll find yourself in prison for assault. Of all the stupid ways of ending up in prison, I've always considered hitting people to be the most stupid.'

Swan said, 'I've always found it to be pretty effective in getting people to do the things you want them to do.'

'It'll be effective in getting you thrown out of this school,' David Gates said angrily. 'I mean that, boy. Even if you can't show any remorse, you might *pretend* to. So what's it to be? Do I send you to the headmaster, or do I get your assurance that you'll leave Hatchly alone? Believe me, the head won't be

88

influenced by your record at swimming this time – nor your academic achievements.'

Swan looked up, having forgotten where the argument was leading. He sighed, and said, 'No.'

'No what?'

'No, don't send me to the head. I didn't actually hit him, anyway,' replied Swan, staring hard at his teacher.

'You weren't seen hitting Hatchly, but you *have* hit people in the recent past, Swan – I know. I told you, it's just the first time we've been able to pin you down. And bullying isn't just physical abuse – it's intimidation too. Now, tell me another reason why you shouldn't be expelled.'

There was a long period of silence. before Swan said in a low voice, 'I won't do it again.'

'What? What won't you do again?'

'Bully Hatchly.' He looked up into David Gates's eyes, then seeing something there, added, 'I won't bully any kid.'

'If you do, Swan, that's it – understand?'

'Yes.'

David Gates then turned to Chris and, with just as much anger in his voice, said, 'Why didn't you report this bullying before now?'

Chris was upset at being targeted too. 'I didn't want – it might have made it worse – I don't know . . .'

'Those who allow it to happen, without reporting it, are almost as bad as the bullies. It isn't cowardly not to retaliate when you're being attacked by a stronger boy – or boys – but it is cowardly to keep it to yourself, hoping it will happen to someone else next time, and not you. If Swan, or anyone else, intimidates you again, you report it – you hear?'

'Yes, sir.'

'Now tell Swan how you feel, when he attacks you.'

Chris was so surprised by this request he didn't really know what to say.

'Tell him honestly what your feelings were. Look him in the eyes and tell him. Swan, I want you to look at Hatchly.'

Chris stared into the brown eyes of his enemy and a certain type of anger welled up inside him.

'I felt *sick*,' he said. 'I was scared to come to school. I couldn't think of anything else. It was just in my head all the time. Wouldn't go away. I hated your guts. Lots of kids hate your guts. You think they like you to be a big man, but people hate your guts . . .'

Swan stared, unblinkingly. It was difficult to see whether the words had any impact on him whatsoever. Chris knew that Swan *liked* kids to be scared of him, so what was the point in all this? Swan didn't do it for the adulation, he did it because he enjoyed the exercise of *power*. If you admitted to him that he had power over you, he would turn you into his slave. Swan didn't want to be a pop star, he wanted to be *king*.

However, Chris let rip with his feelings, and then eventually fell quiet.

'Right,' said David Gates. 'Get out, both of you. I'm not going to ask you to shake hands, or any of that twaddle. It's clear you can't stand the sight of one another. I don't care if you never speak to one another again – I'd just better not hear of any bullying. Don't forget, Swan, if there's any more bullying, you'll go. It'd be a great shame because you're among my brightest lads, you and Hatchly. One of you is chucking it all away on an ego problem, the other one . . .' He stared at Chris. 'Well, I think you've lost your way, old son. Shape up, *both* of you. And, Hatchly, don't forget Mr Leggitt.'

Outside the classroom, Swan muttered under his breath, barely audible even to Chris walking next to him, '*I rule the playground – me* . . . I rule it . . .'

Chris could not care less whether Jason Swan was crowned king of the whole world. He had other worries for the moment. There was Leggitt to think about. Leggo could be quite a formidable swine when he wanted to be. And Chris knew the policy of the school. Leggo would call his mother and tell her that he had been absent without permission. So there was Sally's disappointment in him to think about as well. It was going to be a long hard week.

He sought solace in thoughts of Emily. The more he thought about her, the nicer she seemed. She *was* pretty. There was something about her warm smile which made him feel good. And she liked *him*. Even though they had only seen each other twice – once through glass – she liked him. That was amazing. That was really something. So what if she did talk plummy. She was *class*. Nothing wrong with that.

9

At Emily's request, Anne and Charlotte did not tell their mother or father about Chris's visit. Secrets were an accepted part of the household fare. They made what was otherwise a very dull life exciting. They protected people from the wrath of others. Only James Craster would have denied the high status of secrets in the house, though he himself indulged in the same activity. Of course, secrets could be passed on at any time, to another party, though they were rarely made public.

Emily had spent a feverish time, thinking and planning what she was going to do next. It was all very well promising the boy to write to him, but there were practical difficulties to overcome. It all required careful scheming, and for this Emily needed help. She first recruited her older sister to her cause, swearing her to secrecy.

Charlotte had not wanted to be enlisted in Emily's rebel army, but Emily had pleaded with her. Despite the 'Fanny Price' in Charlotte, she was too honourable and loyal to her sisters to denounce Emily to her father. It had not occurred to Charlotte that dear Em might want her to participate in order to ensure her silence, but it was something of which Emily was certainly capable, in order to achieve her ends.

Anne, too, caught something of the febrile atmosphere and demanded to be involved. Emily told her that she would make sure Anne had a part to play, but for the moment it was only to do with writing letters. Anne was not interested in writing letters, but asked to be kept informed of developments.

The girls all knew they were playing with fire, especially Emily who was the ringleader, but so little in the way of excitement entered their lives that, once caught in the currents of intrigue, they were willing to be carried into the maelstrom, even if it meant severe punishment. Even Charlotte's scruples were buried under Emily's enthusiasm. They used words like 'tryst' and 'liaison' with enthusiasm, never having had the opportunity to speak of such things until now.

Emily was helped by Charlotte in composing a letter to the new pen-friend.

Dear Sir, began the letter, for in her excitement and anxiousness in obtaining the address, Emily had omitted to ask the young man's name.

> *It was so kind of you to visit our house on Monday last and my sister Anne and I very much enjoyed meeting you. You did not see my dear eldest sister, Charlotte, but she too sends her kindest regards. We are only sorry that the circumstances are such that it would be unwise of you to call on us a third time, since our parents do not encourage visitors, wishing to protect us from potential harm. This is no reflection on you as a gentleman, but merely upon the world in general.*
>
> *Sir, you expressed a desire to walk with me.*

(He had not, but Emily felt sure that this was the intention of the visit and the invitation would have been forthcoming, had there been more time and less worry about the intervention of adults). *Please do not think me too forward in accepting your invitation so swiftly, but on Saturday next Papa is taking Mamma to a London doctor, at Southend Hospital, and we shall have the opportunity to meet and talk once again without disturbing them in the least. (Poor, dearest Mamma suffers from her nerves). Perhaps you would be kind enough to meet me at the ford at ten o'clock, where I shall be glad of your company along the dyke?*
I remain, sir, your obedient servant,
Emily Craster.

'Em,' said Charlotte, once they had sealed the envelope and addressed it to 'The Young Master', followed by the address which Emily had obtained, 'perhaps you should not be meeting this boy? You know how angry it will make Papa. We have had a fine game, but shouldn't we leave it here?'

Emily saw that Charlotte was beginning to weaken in her resolve to assist her in her enterprise, but 'Dear Em' was made of stronger material than her elder sister.

'Are you envious, Charlotte?'

'I'm *worried* about you, Em. Oh, of course I'm envious of your courage. I wish I had such fire in me. But I'm not envious of you meeting this boy. I suppose I should be, but I'm not. Just don't do this for our sakes either, Em. There are other ways of bringing excitement into our lives.'

94

'Tell me of one,' challenged Emily.

There was a streak of stubbornness that ran through Emily, which was unyielding. This was her chance to assert herself, to make the sun spin around the earth for a day, rather than always, always obeying the scientific laws of the universe. Father was head of the household, his authority absolute, but his daughter had a will of her own, which might require subterfuge and cunning to realise, but it was not going to be snuffed out because a weak sister was suddenly having second thoughts.

Emily, who knew her sisters wanted to feed second-hand on her adventure, almost as much as she wanted that adventure herself, did know how angry it would make her father. She had felt dreadfully *forward* when she had asked for the boy's address, and still did so, initiating this walk, but she was desperate for some kind of change in her life. Although she loved her father and mother dearly, she felt imprisoned in the farmhouse, and wanted to meet others of her own age.

The only children with whom the girls ever came into contact were two cousins, a brother and sister, who visited once every two years. Those cousins were so terrified of James Craster, who drilled into them before each visit that they were not to upset the sisters with rubbish about the modern world, they were tongue-tied. It was difficult to get a single word out of them, the whole weekend they were there.

Emily wanted to meet this boy who had fallen like an angel from the clouds into their life. He was good-looking, presentable, and though he spoke

95

rather roughly he was a good deal more genteel than Daniel Selby. Emily felt that they would get on famously.

Anne said, 'You must tell us everything he says – every word, mind. I do so want to hear what people of today have to say about the world. Perhaps Papa is wrong about it? We don't know, do we? I should like to ask this boy dozens of questions – hundreds of questions.'

'Perhaps you ought to go instead of me?' suggested Emily, teasing her sister.

Anne looked horrified. 'Meet a boy? Ughhh!'

'Don't be vulgar, Anne,' said Charlotte. 'Boys are not natterjacks. For my part, I should like to speak to him about certain things, but I have no desire actually to visit places beyond Rattan Island. I leave that to the great adventurer, Emily Craster...'

'Then Anne shall be my chaperone, if she is well enough,' said Emily, clasping her hands to her breast. 'For I know you should dislike such a duty, dear Charlotte. Anne and I have often walked as far as the ford together and she will not mind accompanying me to the waterside.'

Charlotte retorted rather sharply, 'Anne will be well enough. She always is if there is some interesting treat in store.'

Emily used a postage stamp from her father's desk drawer. 'I shall give the letter to Daniel Selby, for him to post.'

After lessons the next morning, Emily slipped out to find Dan Selby, who was in the cowshed.

Dan Selby looked up when someone opened the stable door and smiled to himself on seeing Emily Craster. Emily was his favourite. They were a queer lot, these lasses, but Emily was the best of them. She never treated him as if he were a servant, or was some sort of gypsy who had got lost and been taken in. She was straight and up front. Emily held out a letter to him and he wiped his hands on his trousers and reached for it, wondering if it was for him and why it had come to the farm and not to his home address.

'I wonder if you'd be kind enough to post this letter?' said Emily, smiling. 'It's to be a secret between us of course, though Anne and Charlotte know.'

Dan looked at the letter and realised then that it was not for him after all, but for a 'young master'. He pinched the white envelope between thumb and forefinger, holding it on the very corner, to prevent his dirty hands from leaving prints. He stared at it, worried by its existence.

'I don't think I can do this,' Dan said, the letter still dangling from his thumb and forefinger. 'I might get the sack if your dad found out.'

The idea that Dan might not join the conspiracy had obviously not occurred to Emily. Her smooth, shining face suddenly crumpled and the sparkle went out of her eyes. She stared at him as if he had just told her that a favourite pet had died. Tears, he knew, were close behind.

'Your dad wouldn't like this,' he tried to explain. 'He wouldn't like it at all.'

Emily still said nothing. She looked utterly devastated.

'What if he found out?' Dan said, melting a little. Emily was not only his favourite on Haworth Farm, she was the only one out of the whole bunch that he had any time for at all.

Emily clasped her hands together and said anxiously. 'He won't find out – ever. I promise.'

Dan shrugged. And if the worst came to the worst, so what if he did get the sack? Would that be the end of the world? It might even be a chance to make the break.

He stuffed the letter in his inside pocket.

'If he does,' he said, 'I'm for the high jump, young woman, and no mistake. One thing's certain, he'll not find another man around these parts as 'ud work under his conditions, so we're probably stuck with one another anyways. Go on, off with you. I'll put it through the door. The stamp's not enough for the post . . .'

'Thank you, Daniel – oh, *thank* you,' cried Emily.

Once more her eyes sparkled. Once more her face shone. Dan sighed. Why did he take these risks? And for a snip of a girl? Was it just for a pretty face and a smile? Maybe it was because he loathed James Craster so much. Over the years Dan had endured much verbal abuse and he had come to despise his employer a great deal, regarding him with a deep contempt. James Craster was a hypocrite who pretended to be high, fine gentry, when Dan knew that the farmer came from ordinary labouring stock like himself and had married into money.

That evening, Dan paid a visit to the Plough and Sail at Paglesham Eastend. It was some time since he had visited this pub, but even so most people at the bar knew him. As well as being a farm-hand

Dan Selby was a sexton at three local churches, one of them being at Paglesham Churchend.

'Evenin' Dan,' said the bartender. 'Bitter?'

Dan nodded, scratching his unshaven chin with grimy nails.

'Ta, Jim,' he said, lifting the pint to his lips.

Once he had quenched his thirst, Dan took the letter out of his coat pocket. Now that he was away from the farm and out of the influence of Emily's girlish charms, he was inclined to throw the letter on the pub fire. He stared at the address for a moment, then called Jim over.

'Who lives at this place?' he asked the barman, showing him the front of the envelope.

There were only twenty houses in Paglesham Eastend and Jim knew the occupants of every one of them.

'Youngish, divorced woman,' said Jim. 'Sally Hatchly.'

'No one else.'

Jim shrugged. 'She's got a son – boy of about fourteen or fifteen.'

Dan knew this was the 'Young Master.'

'Good-lookin' boy, is he?' asked Dan. 'I mean, the sort girls might go doolally over?'

Jim looked thoughtful. 'I dunno about that. He's a nice enough lad, so far as I know.'

Dan nodded and put the letter back into his pocket. So that was it, he thought, but where would young Emily have seen the Hatchly boy? Suddenly, Dan remembered the footprint in the cowpat and he laughed out loud, causing one or two faces to turn his way and smile. Yes, the footprint! That cheeky young tyke had come out to the farm when he and Craster were out in the fields.

'He must have a lot o' gall,' said Dan to himself, taking a good long pull on his pint. 'He deserves a letter.'

After several pints Dan left the pub. The freezing air pinched at his red-veined face, but Dan Selby was impervious to anything the British weather could throw at him.

Behind the pub was a little row of cottages. Dan found the right one and slipped the letter through the door.

There, it was done, and James Craster could dance on a silage heap for all Dan Selby cared!

PART THREE

A Contract of True Love

10

'A letter for you,' said Sally, when Chris came down to breakfast on Thursday morning. 'At least I *think* it's for you – I'm certainly not *the young master.*' She grinned.

Chris blinked and took the letter, wondering if it was some kind of joke. Perhaps Swan had thought of a devious way of getting his own back? Chris tore open the envelope.

He read the letter twice, with great astonishment and just a little lack of understanding in places, while Sally stared at him the whole time. Either it was a joke, or the girl really wrote as she spoke, like someone out of *Pride and Prejudice.* Chris recalled how intensely eager the girl had been and he was inclined to think the letter meant what it said. He stuffed it back into the envelope again, quickly, aware that he was going red.

Sally looked at him aghast. 'Aren't you going to tell me who it's from?'

Chris burned. 'It's from a girl, you know that, or you wouldn't be interested.'

Sally placed a hand over her heart and looked hurt. 'My darling child, I'm interested in *anything* to do with you.'

Chris nodded and to change the subject said, 'In

that case, I bunked off school on Monday. I'm supposed to tell you, before Leggo rings you.'

Sally's face sagged a little. His ruse worked. Sally appeared to lose interest in the letter immediately. 'Oh, Chrissie – what did you do that for?'

'Got fed up.'

'But you can't just bunk off school every time you get fed up, Chris. Did you get into trouble? Did you have to do lines or something?'

He nodded again. 'Had to do extra work. They don't give you lines now, they give you extra work.'

'Where did you go? To the pictures?'

'No, I just went for a walk – over at Barling. I needed to get some fresh air, Mum. I needed to think a bit.'

'But *why* did you get fed up at school?'

'Lots of reasons. David Gates was getting at me. And Swan had another go at me too. Dad saw him grab me after school and he told him off. I think it was Dad who rang the school and told them, even though I said not to.'

Sally looked indignant. 'I should think he would. I'm glad your father has at least got the sense to do things like that. I should have done something about it myself, a long time ago.' Her eyes opened a little wider. 'That time you came home with a split lip and a black eye – you said you got that falling down in rugby. Was that this boy . . .?'

Chris shrugged and remained silent, thereby confirming Sally's fears.

'Why do I let you talk me into doing nothing?' cried Sally, exasperated. 'Don't you know your father uses things like this as ammunition? He says I can't take care of you.'

104

'I see – not worried about me getting beat up – just about Dad,' grumbled Chris.

'That's not fair,' said Sally, close to tears.

Chris relented. 'Well, I didn't want you to, because I hoped it would go away and there wouldn't be any need. Anyway, it usually makes things worse when parents butt in. Parents and teachers are only around some of the time. Swan reckons he rules the playground, and he's right. What he means is, when you lot aren't there to protect us, *he's* the king. No matter how much you want to look after me, Mum, there's always the chance people like Swan will get me alone . . .'

'The only way to stop this kind of thing,' said Sally furiously, 'is to use authority. You can't use authority by keeping it to yourself and allowing it to happen. If he so much as *touches* you again, you report him, you hear? It's all so stupid, this macho idea that you shouldn't tell.'

Chris nodded, thinking he probably would, now.

Sally sipped her tea and stared at him while he poured milk on his cornflakes.

'What about drugs and things,' she asked. 'Do you get offered drugs?'

'I don't have anything to do with that,' Chris said honestly.

'You know Mrs Raven lost her boy? He drowned himself off Leigh. That was drugs.'

'Mum, I don't have anything to do with that. I don't even smoke, for crying out loud. I had a can of beer once, that was all.'

'Beer?' She sat up straight in her chair. 'Where did you get it?'

'One of the older kids got it from the supermarket. Mum,' said Chris evenly, 'you don't think I'm going to become an alchy after what I've seen happen to Dad, do you? Relax. Let me eat my cornflakes. I can't even eat my breakfast without getting grilled by the FBI. I had it *once*, that was all. I'm telling you about it, aren't I?'

Sally's stiff body gradually relaxed. 'I'm sorry, Chrissie. Of course I worry about you, I'm bound to, aren't I? I don't suppose you're an angel and I wouldn't want you to be. Just stay away from drugs and I'll be happy.'

Chris sighed and took the letter from Emily out of his pocket. 'So it's all right to get a girl pregnant, is it?' he said, staring at the unfranked envelope.

Sally's head jerked up. 'What?'

He grinned at her. 'Had you there, Mum. Which reminds me – it's human biology class today. Facts of life and all that. We had a film on AIDS last time. Enough to scare the orcs out of you, isn't it?'

'Orcs?' said Sally, faintly.

'Yeah, orcs – as in Dungeons and Dragons. Really, Mum, you can be *boring* sometimes.'

'You mean ignorant, don't you? Not boring,' Sally replied, only gradually recovering from the shock of his joke.

'No, *boring*. Boring means lots of different things. Boring doesn't just mean boring.'

Sally shook her head in bewilderment. 'I suppose we had our own language when I was your age, but I'm sure it wasn't as confusing as the language of kids today. You seem to be economising on words, rather than adding to the vocabulary. Using ordinary word to make ten others. We were invented words – like *dinky-dink* – that

106

meant something was great. Or *yonks* meant a long time . . .'

'Things are different now,' insisted Chris.

'Yes,' said Sally, sighing. 'Now there's drugs and AIDS and all sorts of horrors waiting to trap our children.'

'And terrible haircuts, pierced ears, tattoos – oh, the horrors preying on the young today!' cried Chris in a high shrill voice.

She got up and hugged his head, making him feel uncomfortable.

He pulled away when he could do so without hurting her feelings. 'Oh, Mum, don't get heavy on me, that's *boring*.'

They finished breakfast and then watched the news on TV before getting ready to leave the house. When they were in the car, on the way to school and work, Sally said, 'You know, Chris, I'm sure it was a good joke, but it's not funny for a girl to get pregnant in her teenage years. It sets her back for a long time – sometimes for life.'

'It happened to you, didn't it?' said Chris. 'But you're all right, Mum.'

'Am I?' said Sally, grimly.

He put an arm around her and squeezed her. 'I think you are. It's great having a young mum. We can talk about things. We can smoke and drink beer together . . .'

'No more jokes,' said Sally. 'I'm a shattered woman after today's little talk.'

Chris laughed. He was in a good mood. That girl wanted to see him again. It was something to look forward to. Something a bit out of the ordinary. A bit *weird*.

On Saturday morning, Chris rose early. He read again that amazing letter. It was brilliant. She wrote the way she talked. Still wearing his pyjamas, he propped the letter against his computer, while he battled with orcs and giants, poisonous dwarves and monsters from the id. Once he had out-fenced a few of his adversaries on the screen, he felt set up for the day.

When the bright, garish colours on the VDU began to make him feel fuzzy-headed, he went downstairs and watched the programme he had videoed the previous evening.

It was a new soap called *Blackmore's Wharf*, about trawler-fishing families in Norfolk. Captains of trawlers, their crews and their families were having confrontations every few minutes on the TV screen. Boats were lost in the ocean, sabotage abounded, and supermarket fish magnates cheated the hard-working, hard-living fishermen. There was love and death, hatred and grief. Chris got bored after a while, after seeing too many baskets of fish thrown overboard, and too many wives screaming at each other in the market-place. He preferred the action on the high seas to people scrapping on and around the harbour. He switched over to the cartoons on another channel.

Sally came downstairs and told him off for watching too much TV, but she did not switch it off. Instead she made herself a strong cup of coffee and sat watching it too.

'I'm going shopping this morning – want to come?' she asked him during the advertisements.

'No thanks. Going for a walk.'

'Anywhere special?' asked Sally.

He played it casually. 'Thought I might go and see if they're catching any fish, out by – by Rattan Island.'

Sally raised her eyebrows. 'Fishing? In this weather? Isn't the river still iced over?'

Chris kicked himself mentally. 'Well, it's *beginning* to thaw. Some of the kids are going out there with their dads, today. I just thought I'd go along and see.' He knew the word *dads* would make Sally feel guilty that he, Chris, did not have one of those in the home and, as he had guessed, it stopped her from enquiring any further.

Sally shrugged. 'Suit yourself, buster, but wrap up warm. It's still minus a million on the marshes. You'll need your scarf and gloves on, as well.'

Wrap up well? Scarf and gloves? How could he wrap up well? He wanted to look cool. Emily had seen him in his school uniform, which was naff. Today, he was going dressed as *him*. If he wore a load of clothes, he'd look and *feel* like a Michelin Man. He wanted to be – exc*ep*tional!

He went upstairs and washed, then back to his bedroom to choose his clothes carefully.

The Levi jeans were obligatory of course and everything else was fashioned around them. With the Levis went a thick leather belt made in the Czech Republic prior to the collapse of communism. There were red stars stitched around the holes. The belt also included friendship bands (woven by Chris himself, last summer) looped on the left side of the brass buckle. The friendship bands' design was a copy of a Cherokee Indian blanket pattern he had found on a postcard from an aunt.

A Joe Bloggs shirt was chosen as the first top layer. He decided that, over the shirt, he would have on a Gasoline Alley sweater: a loose one that looked crumpled and well used. On top of all these he would have the All American brown leather jacket that made him look broad-shouldered.

Reebok trainers went on his feet.

A large-billed cap bearing the words GREEN BAY PACKERS on the front was worn the way the manufacturers expected it to be: with the bill pointing forwards. It had just become boring to wear caps back to front.

Once these items adorned his body, he stood in front of the mirror and studied himself for at least half an hour. Next he put some gel on his hair and spent a quarter of an hour shaping it into what he considered a pretty near equivalent of the style worn by Tom Cruise in his latest movie. Had Emily seen his preparations she would think it was like the arming of the hero in the age of chivalry.

He was ready to meet his date and asked Sally for a lift to Barling, which was not on her way to anywhere she wanted to go, but she obliged her son anyway.

'You'll freeze in those clothes. Where's the scarf and gloves I mentioned?'

'Aw, Mum . . .'

'I know,' she said, starting the car. 'Don't be boring.'

Chris sat back in the car after that, saying nothing, lost in his own thoughts. He wondered what he was going to say to the girl. The old familiar knot in his stomach was telling him it would not be easy. He didn't understand why he couldn't just relax with girls, treat them as he did his mates? Mates were easy to talk to. Girls weren't *that* much different, were they? Yet he knew this one was. This one was *quite* different.

He hunched in his seat, watching the scenery fly by the car window, trying to combat his tenseness by humming a tune. The excitement kept surging through him, though, and it was all he could do to stop himself from blurting the whole thing out to Sally. He was sure she would have understood his agitation, but for some reason he felt shy about telling his mum he was going to meet a girl. Would she make fun of him? Probably not, but he was feeling too vulnerable to risk any kidding from his mum, even gentle stuff.

He would tell Sally *afterwards*, when it was all over.

11

Anne was a kestrel today.

She had looked out of her bedroom window on waking and had seen a kestrel hovering above a dyke. The birds of prey liked the dykes because the grass was kept short on the crown by walkers. Mice and other small creatures had little cover if they decided it was necessary to cross the top of the dyke, so the hawks and falcons cruised the snaking wall, watching for any opportunist creature making a dash for it.

When the kestrel stooped, Anne was inside it. She soared away afterwards, into the pale blue sky. She was free – free to fly where she wished. She looked back and saw Haworth Farm, a black collection of small boxes on the ground, and felt sorry for her sisters still trapped inside them. But she, Anne Craster, was going to cross oceans and earths, see many wondrous sights, hear many strange tales, follow many secret paths. Hers was to be a life of adventure, while poor Emily and Charlotte lived the life of drudges, staring up into the greyness, envying their youngest sister, who was brave enough to . . .

'Anne? What are you doing?'

Anne snapped out of her reverie instantly. 'I don't feel very well today, Mamma,' she said. She glanced out of the window at a rotting tree stump on the edge of the marshes. 'It feels like there's a fungus growing inside me.'

Hannah Craster sighed heavily. She loved her daughters dearly, but they seemed to be slipping out of her control. When James and she had first decided to go ahead with their plan to lock out the twentieth century, it was Hannah's intention to send the girls to university, perhaps in France or Italy where they would not be so much of an oddity. She felt by then they would have reached a point in their maturity where they could cope with the modern world. However, over the subsequent years, James had become iron in his resolve not to allow them to leave the farm until they were much older, and would not listen to any arguments to the contrary. He simply refused to discuss it.

Hannah's attention returned to her youngest daughter. 'Really, Anne, I do wish you'd *try* to fight this illness. Your father and I have to go away today and I can't leave you if you're feeling unwell again.'

Saturday. Today was the day that the boy was coming to take Emily for a walk. She could not disappoint her sister on a day like today. There was excitement in the air. Today the hawk might fly just a little way beyond the farm. Today there was a little freedom in the wind.

'I think I shall be fine, Mamma. It's just a passing fever, I'm sure. Once I get up and have some break-fast, I'm sure I'll feel a lot better.'

'It's the atmosphere around this farm,' grumbled Hannah. 'I'm positive these bouts of illness you get are marsh fever, whatever Dr Stacey says. There must be all sorts of bad humours coming from those muddy creeks. We need to live in an isolated place, it's true, but it certainly isn't healthy.'

'I'm sure you're right, Mamma.'

Her two sisters were already at the breakfast table, eating toast and marmalade. At least, Emily had marmalade on her toast, but Charlotte was eating hers dry. There was not even any butter on Charlotte's toast.

'Don't you like marmalade any more?' asked Anne of Charlotte. 'You used to like it a lot.'

Emily said, 'It's *because* she likes it that she's not eating it, isn't it, Charlotte dear?'

Hannah stared at her daughters. 'What nonsense,' she said. 'Charlotte just doesn't feel like eating marmalade today.'

Charlotte said nothing, but ate her dry toast with a stoical expression on her face. She and Emily shared a secret this morning. The secret was that Charlotte had woken in the middle of the night with the frights: not just with the *frights* but sweating in terror of something . . . she didn't know what.

She only knew it had something to do with this boy that Emily was meeting.

It had been impossible for her to stay in her own room alone with her night fears, with dark, sinister shapes of furniture around her, watching her, waiting for her to fall asleep again, and the walls moving closer to her bed, and things at the window rustling, whispering her name over and over. So she crept along the landing to dear Em's room and crawled into bed with her, hugging her for comfort. Emily barely woke, murmured something unintelligible, and then fell fast asleep again.

Papa would not have approved of his eldest

daughter being so afraid that she needed her younger sister for comfort.

This morning, on returning to her own room, Charlotte had had to change her sheets and pillow-slips before her mother came in to see her and despaired at her 'lack of control'. They were still soaked with her perspiration, the room being too cold for them to dry. Charlotte had hidden the wet sheets under the bed, planning to wash them while her mamma and papa were away today, and then to dry them in front of the fire.

'I think it's admirable that Charlotte disciplines herself,' said Emily. 'Charlotte's spirit triumphs over her worldly desires – isn't that so, Charlotte?'

'Nonsense,' repeated her mother. 'Charlotte merely shows restraint, where you are perhaps a little indulgent, Emily. You might do better to copy her good example. A little less marmalade would do you no harm at all.'

Hannah smiled fondly at her eldest daughter. There was a warmth between the two which was not in the least envied by Emily. She thought it nice that her mother and her elder sister were good friends.

Emily turned to Anne. 'Are you feeling well today, Anne dear? No bad tummy troubles?'

'Thank you, I'm feeling quite all right now,' said Anne, taking Charlotte's share of the marmalade as well as her own. 'I was feeling *slightly* poorly when I woke, but Mamma came and cheered me up, didn't you, Mamma? The consequence is, I feel quite well altogether.'

Charlotte said drily, 'It's amazing what a mother can do, just by being there, isn't it?'

James Craster strode into the room. He had been out doing the early morning chores long before the girls had stirred. He sat down at the table. A plate of bacon, eggs, fried tomatoes and mushrooms was placed before him. He alone had a cooked breakfast. He was the man of the house. On his shoulders rested the responsibility of the family. Such responsibility required square meals to sustain the bearer.

'What's this about mothers?' he asked, after the third mouthful had been swallowed.

'We were just saying,' said Charlotte in a completely different tone of voice to the one she used before, 'how Mamma is an example to us all.'

'What sort of example?' he asked, looking up.

'Her self-sacrifice. She is always a wife and a mother first,' said Charlotte, 'and then a woman with needs.'

James Craster frowned. 'Needs? I supply all your mother's needs.'

'Of course you do, dear,' said Hannah quickly. 'Charlotte doesn't realise what she's saying.'

'You must understand, Charlotte,' said James Craster, waving his fork, 'that women like your mother require a lot of support from a man. However, they need little else, *but* that support. Now, I will have a bit less chatter at the table. When I was your age I wasn't allowed to speak at all during meals – we're beginning to turn the meal table into a zoo.'

There was silence for a few moments, then Emily dared to continue the subject. 'I think we should tell Mamma if we admire her, Papa. That isn't idle chatter, is it?'

James Craster's face turned to stone. 'Emily, you

116

were always the most wilful of children. If your mother needs admiration, *I* shall be the one to supply it. Fortunately she's not of a frivolous turn of mind – unlike her daughter – and therefore needs no such flattery from me.'

Emily was upset by this remark. 'I am *not* frivolous, Papa.'

'You have a head full of cotton wool, child.' He waved his fork again. 'Do you think I haven't seen you staring out of that bedroom window of yours, dreaming of heaven knows what, lost in some silly fantasy? You should be more like your sister Charlotte – she has a serious turn of mind. Look at your studies. Your grasp of mathematics is appalling. Or lack of grasp, I should say.'

'Oh, come now, James, she's not that bad . . .' began Hannah, quietly, but was silenced with another wave of the fork.

'Let the girl speak for herself,' he commanded.

Emily was close to tears now, despite an inner resolve not to show her father that she was upset.

'But my other studies are all very good,' she said, her lip trembling. 'My English studies . . .'

'Your other studies are not what I'm talking about. They are as good as they are. It's your mathematics I'm speaking about. It's no good being brilliant at one thing, you have to strive to be above average at *everything*. If you miss one, you *fail* overall. That's what I mean about frivolous thinking. You're too easily satisfied with being good at one thing and everything else can go to pot, can't it?'

'That's not fair,' said Hannah. 'She does try.'

James Craster began eating again. 'I know what's

117

fair and what isn't, Hannah. Let me be the judge of my own daughter's abilities, if you please. You have your views, I have mine. I simply wish they were compatible, that's all. But if you have to take Emily's side against me, that's up to you.'

'I wasn't . . .' began Hannah.

'Enough,' he interrupted with some anger in his voice. 'Can't a man have his meal in peace, without all this?'

After that remark, no one else spoke.

At nine o'clock Hannah and James Craster were taken off in the pony and trap by Dan Selby to Rochford railway station. Dan was having Chervil, the pony, shod while in Rochford. The girls had been told to get on with whatever they wished, so long as they were not idle.

Emily immediately went up to her room to change into walking clothes. She planned to wear a thick, tartan skirt, a Fair Isle jumper and lace-up boots. Of these items, only the toes of the boots would be visible anyway, since she had a heavy Irish shawl-coat which would cover her from neck to ankles to go over the top. A scarlet silk headscarf sent her by an aunt would add a dash of colour. Emily knew it was very daring of her to wear the red scarf, but she knew that it would contrast dramatically with her black hair.

Finally, she found the muff her mother had given her as a six-year-old.

Charlotte came to her room while she was dressing.

'Emily,' said Charlotte, 'I'm beginning to think this is a very bad idea . . .'

'Oh, you, Fanny Price,' laughed Emily.

'No, really, Em. You don't know this boy. We don't even know his name.'

Emily turned to face her eldest sister. 'But that's just it, Charlotte.' Emily clasped her hands together and looked at the ceiling. 'I *want* to know him, Charlotte. I want to know what a boy like him thinks, and how he feels about – oh, *life*. We've never met anyone like him before, have we? I'm sure Papa's right about fickle young men, but perhaps some of them aren't so fickle? Perhaps some of them are good, kind, thoughtful young men? I want to find out for myself.

'I once saw a boy canoeing along our creek. He waved to me. I was only twelve then, but I'm not happy with just waving any longer, Charlotte. I have to talk with one of them. Oh, don't look so glum,' laughed Emily, 'I'm only going for a little stroll along the dyke. I shan't even lose sight of the farm. Anne will be with me. What can possibly happen to us in that short time?'

Charlotte actually wrung her hands. 'I don't know, but my stomach keeps turning over. What if Papa finds out? He'll be so dreadfully angry, you know. He – he can be very fierce-tempered at times.'

'Well, I don't care,' said Emily firmly. 'By then I shall have spoken with my – my *beau* – and whatever punishment Papa feels necessary, I shall accept with good grace.'

At five minutes to ten, Emily and Anne strolled down the cockleshell path to Rattan Hard. The frozen shells crunched beneath their feet. Seagulls with the eyes of pirates stood on either side and watched them pass.

Above, the heavens were still a very pale blue,

with wisps of cloud just stroking the underside of the sky. A chill wind was cutting in from the seaward side engrained with the salt smell of ocean spray. The creeks lined with saltwort and bladderwort were uncovered. In the summer they would have overpowered all around them with their organic smell of putrefying shellfish and plant life, but the winter held their odours in check.

From the hard, old wrecks looking like prehistoric carcasses, bits of rotten rope dangling from their crumbling beams, could be seen either sinking in or emerging from the slick mud. Brent geese fed in, on and around them. A tidal race was beginning to sweep through the channels, chasing the dunlin higher up the steep banks of the U-shaped troughs. There was a clarity to the air which made the morning seem especially young.

Emily, her hands buried deep in her muff, saw the boy standing on the far side of the hard. Her heart began to run ahead of her breathing. She swallowed quickly, before speaking to her sister.

'There he is,' she whispered to Anne. 'Come on, let's cross the hard quickly before the water gets too deep.'

Anne looked stricken. 'Em,' she said. 'How will we get back if the tide's in?'

'It doesn't get deep enough to go past one's knees, silly. It's a ford. If we get wet when we come back, it doesn't really matter. We can change our boots, once we get home.'

'I thought we were going to stay *this* side. We have never left Papa's land,' insisted Anne.

'He might be frightened to come over here. This is Papa's land after all. We must go to him.'

Anne stood her ground, her little figure shivering. 'No, I'm staying here. I'll chaperone you from here, Em. You go over and I'll watch you from this side.'

Emily stared at her sister for a moment. She was not going to have her plans thwarted by a sister who was concerned about a little bit of water.

'All right, Anne dear, you stay on this side of the creek and I'll wave to you every so often, to let you know I'm all right. Is that understood? You must watch me closely from here – and try not to get too cold. Walk around or skip.'

'I haven't got a skipping rope.'

'I mean, without a rope,' Emily said, wondering if her sister was being deliberately obstructive.

Anne nodded briskly, still looking worried. Emily kissed her on the cheek and then began to cross the swiftly flowing water. Under her feet was a metre of hard core, which raised the level of the ford above the mud of the creek. At the moment the water hardly reached the top of her thick soles. She could see creatures in its ripples, crossing the shallows. The hard was just fifty or so metres wide and she was soon across and striding confidently towards the young man.

12

'Hello,' he said, awkwardly. 'You all right then?'

Emily stared at his peculiar clothes. She had never seen her father and Daniel Selby in anything like them. Whether she liked them or not, she hadn't decided.

'Hello.' She offered her hand for him to shake and he took it awkwardly, letting it drop almost immediately he touched it. 'I'm so glad you could come,' she added. 'I've been looking forward to our meeting all week. I hope you did not mind the fact that I was the one to arrange this outing?'

He stuck his hands in the pockets of his blue , shapeless trousers. 'What, me? I'm all for this feminist stuff. I like a girl with a bit of bottle.'

Bottle? She felt herself colouring up. Was he referring to her ankles? Her ankles were thicker than Charlotte's, but then Charlotte was *so* thin. Once, when Charlotte was angry with her, she had called Emily 'bottle legs', which had hurt her dreadfully. Now Emily was very sensitive about ankles.

'What's the matter?' he said. 'What've I said?'

He looked concerned. She doubted an insult was intended.

'Nothing, nothing at all. Shall we walk along the dyke?'

'If you like.'

The dyke path was just wide enough for them to walk side by side. Emily turned just before they set off, to wave to Anne, who gave her a little wave back. Then Emily concentrated on where to put her feet, because the grassy crown of the dyke was quite slippery. She noticed her shawl-coat was getting wet at the bottom, from touching the long grass, but there was nothing she could do about that.

'You see *Blackmore's Wharf* this week? I think it's going off a bit.'

'I don't understand,' she said.

'Telly – the new soap.' He looked across at her as he spoke. 'Haven't you seen it?'

She was mystified by this attempt at an explanation and threw a look of mild panic at him.

'Last night,' he said, sounding exasperated. 'It was the fourth episode. Don't you watch telly on Fridays?'

Fridays?

'On Friday evenings,' she told him, 'we read poetry to the whole family – all except Papa, that is, for he's quite hopeless at anything requiring intonation. Yesterday evening I read 'The Poplar Field' by Mr Cowper. You must know it: *The poplars are fell'd; farewell to the shade, and the whispering sound of the cool colonnade . . .*? Charlotte gave us a really spirited 'Battle of the Baltic' by Thomas Campbell, and Mamma and Anne read 'The Forsaken Merman', with Anne doing the refrains.'

He stared at her, blankly. It gave her the opportunity to ask a question the answer to which she had been guessing ever since she had seen him staring through her living-room window.

'Would you mind telling me your name?'

'What?' he said, coming to life. He took off his cap and put it on backwards. 'Chris.'

'Kris?' she said. 'How romantic. Is that a name from the Indian continent? Or perhaps from the Malay Peninsula? I believe the Malays call their jungle knife the *kris*.'

'No,' he laughed. '*Christopher*. My name's Christopher Hatchly. You've heard of Chris before, haven't you?'

'I've heard of Christopher – there's Christopher Marlowe and Saint Christopher – but not *Chris*.'

'It's short for Christopher.'

'Oh, like *Kit*.'

'Well, that's me,' he said, smiling. 'Kit Hatchly. And you're Emily, right? Can I call you Emma? Like Emma Thompson, the actress? Emma's a great name. You talk really weird, you do. I'd like you to meet Ishwinder. Now his mum and dad *do* come from India – or did. They're all British Sikhs now. They wear turbans, you know? All Sikhs have Singh as their second name – it means lion, or something. Ishwinder's my best mate. I've got my enemies too, though,' he said darkly. 'We've got this kid called Swan at school, who's always thumping people. All I did was look at his girl once and he reckons that's a federal case! From what I hear she puts it about a bit anyway. I mean, she looks like Dracula's sister – dresses up Gothic. One of these days me and Ishwinder are going to jump Swan and knock seven bells out of him – teach him a lesson. Right?'

Gothic. Emily clutched at the one straw which she understood amongst a bale of strange sounds.

'I love that story,' she said, 'of Percy Shelley and

Lord Byron, and Mary Wollstonecraft Shelley, when they all got together in Italy to tell tales, and Mary invented the wonderfully Gothic tale of Dr Frankenstein . . .'

All she seemed to know about was dead poets. Her family obviously didn't own a television.

'What about films?' he asked her. 'Haven't you seen the latest Arnie film, *Wasteland Wars*? You don't know what you're missing. It's great.'

'Films?' she said, helplessly.

'Yeah, you know, movies. The cinema,' he added in exasperation, realising he was missing the mark every time.

'Oh,' her eyes brightened, '*that* kind of film. I was thinking of a thin layer of something, a membrane. I know what you mean now. You mean a strip of celluloid coated with light-sensitive emulsion which, when it's exposed to an optical image in a device known as a *camera*, gives a negative or positive photograph – after it's been treated with chemicals, of course. We know about film. We have to, in case the school inspector asks us questions, though Papa does not approve of such devices as cameras. Family pictures, yes?'

It was Chris's turn to look helpless. He didn't seem to be making the right connections.

'Well, I mean *moving* pictures,' he said.

'Yes, I've heard of those too, but I've never seen any.'

'Oh right. But, look, you do all this singing and stuff. Don't you listen to pop? Do you know any bands? What about Standing Up Strate? Have you heard them?'

'I don't know anything about . . . whatever it is.'

125

'Don't you ever go out anywhere?' he said. 'I mean, which school do you go to?'

Emily said. 'Mamma teaches us at home. Papa doesn't like us mixing with the outside world. He says the twentieth century is a monstrous place . . .'

'S'not a place. It's a *time*,' interrupted Chris with some justification.

'Yes, but Papa has *made* it into a place. If we stay at home, on the island, we can't be touched by the twentieth century. This is the first time I've stepped off the island. Charlotte once went to Southend Hospital, but she was only four at the time and can't remember a great deal about it.'

'The first time off Rattan Island?' Chris stopped, the hairs on his neck standing on end. 'You must be barmy by now.'

'Barmy? Oh, that's slang, isn't it? Papa doesn't encourage slang. He says it undermines the English language.'

'What?' cried Chris.

'It's cant,' replied Emily.

'Never mind *cant*, whatever that is, I mean – surely you've been to Rochford or Southend before?'

'Never. I have never left Rattan Island, except perhaps as a baby or small infant, but I can't remember those times.'

'That's – that's like something out of Dungeons and Dragons, that is. I can't believe it. You've got to be joking. No, no, all right, I can see you're not kidding. Jeez, though!'

'Jeez? Is that more cant?' she laughed.

'What is this flipping cant stuff?'

'Why, the secret language of gypsies, vagabonds

126

and thieves,' she giggled. 'You knew that, surely? You're a little raffish yourself, you know, but I don't mean that as an insult. I find it wickedly attractive. I've always liked the *bad* fairies in stories – they're more interesting. That must be a secret between the two of us, because Papa would not approve.'

He stopped and stared at her. She really was very pretty. He found her ignorance of the world fascinating. It made him feel superior to her. He was the one who knew how the world *really* was, and she had to rely on his knowledge of it. Why, he could tell her anything! Not that he would. Yet she was obviously brilliant at general knowledge and English. She used words he had never heard before. She was, he decided, more intelligent than himself. Well, he could teach her about the outside world. He knew all about *that*.

'Your poncho thing's getting wet on the grass,' he said. 'You'd better pick it up a bit.' He pointed to the hem of her Irish shawl-coat.

'Oh, no, that wouldn't be proper,' she said, mysteriously.

'Right,' he said, as if he knew exactly what she meant.

By this time they had walked quite a long way and had come to a row of houses built at a right angle to the dyke. The road past this terraced row of cottages ended abruptly at the dyke. There was a telephone booth and a bus stop opposite the dwellings, at which a woman with a plastic shopping bag was waiting. The pair on the dyke looked down on this scene and Chris was aware of some consternation within Emily.

'What's the matter,' he asked her. 'Why're you looking like that?'

'She's a woman,' gasped Emily.

Chris looked again, and confirmed this fact. 'So what?'

'But she's – she's wearing *trousers*.'

Chris laughed. 'Those aren't trousers, they're ski pants. Anyway, why shouldn't she wear trousers? My mum wears them all the time. Lots of women do.'

'A lady should not dress in such a fashion,' stated Emily, primly. 'It's quite improper.'

'People are free to do what they like,' Chris said, a little shocked by this bigotry. 'You can't tell other people what to wear.'

As he was saying this, a green single-decker bus appeared in the distance, coming along the long straight road across the flatlands. Chris studied the bemused expression on Emily's face and then said, 'It's going to stop at the bottom. You've never seen a bus before, have you? Come on, come and have a closer look.'

'I don't think I can get down there,' she said.

Chris took her objections as shyness on her part. 'Yeah, come on, you'll be all right.'

With that he grabbed her arm and steered her down the steep bank of the dyke. Her heels skidded on the wet grass and she had to take her left hand out of her muff, to grab him by the arm.

'I'm going to fall,' she said.

'No, you're not, you're all right,' said Chris, enjoying the grip of her hand on his jacket. 'Come on.'

When they reached the bottom of the dyke, the

bus had arrived and was just turning around. Chris took hold of Emily's hand and pulled her over to where it stopped. He climbed on the step after the woman in ski pants and tugged Emily with him.

'Come on,' he said. 'I'll show you some *real* life. Let's take the bus to the seafront. Let's go to the Golden Mile. That'll blow your mind after being on Rattan Island.'

Emily pulled back. 'Oh, no. Please.'

Again, Chris thought she was playing some sort of game with him, but she looked serious.

'Oi, you two!' cried the bus driver. 'On or off?'

Chris ignored the driver and stared at Emily. Why on earth would she object to a short bus ride? Unless of course she hadn't got any money on her? He smiled at her.

'Come on, Emma,' he said. 'It's all right, I'll pay.'

With that he gave her arm a final tug. She would have fallen if he hadn't reached back and caught her. When she regained her feet, she was actually on the bus steps. Chris's hands were on her shoulders, steadying her.

The bus driver rammed the vehicle into gear and put his foot on the accelerator.

''Bout flippin' time,' he grumbled.

The bus began to pull away and Emily found herself bundled into a seat near the front. With panic rising in her breast, she held on tightly to Chris's hand, her breath coming out in short gasps. She felt bewildered and hardly realised what was happening to her.

'Where are we going?' she asked, fearfully.

Chris said, 'I told you – to the seafront. I'll show you the arcades. We can have jellied eels, ice cream, whatever you like. I've got some money, don't worry.'

The bus began to pick up speed, until it was going a great deal faster than she had ever travelled in the pony and trap. Fields flashed by outside the window. She hated the loud noise of the engine. The vibrations and mixed smells of oil, petrol, people and vehicle upholstery made her feel ill. Her stomach began to churn with fear. She clutched Chris's arm with a claw-like grip, until she realised her long nails must be hurting him because he peeled them away with his other hand.

'Hey, watch it,' he laughed. 'You'll ruin my jacket. What are you, a cyborg?'

'I have to go home,' she wailed.

One or two people looked round at them, but seeing teenagers, shook their heads. The bus came to a grinding stop again, its brakes squealing horribly, and she felt some relief. She sat there, recovering for a moment, still trembling from the experience. A woman got on in a mock leopardskin coat and Emily was astounded to see that, under the parted collar of this outer garment, the woman hardly wore anything at all. The tops of her breasts were exposed. Emily looked away quickly, shocked and embarrassed.

Then the bus started pulling away again, before they had time to get off.

'It'll only take half an hour to get there,' Chris said. 'I'll get you back again.'

She spent the next few minutes fighting the nausea.

Chris stared at her, realising she was feeling sick.

Her face was wan and dark rings had appeared around her eyes.

'Here, have some gum,' he said, offering her some spearmint chewing gum, 'it'll make you feel better. It always does me, when I get car sick.'

He peeled the paper off the gum and handed it to her. She chewed it once, then swallowed it whole. Chris stared at her in disbelief, remembering now that she had probably never seen chewing gum before. Perhaps it had not been a good idea to get her on the bus? If she was going to be sick all over the place, there might be some sort of a row.

When they came into the edge of the town, into the residential areas, Emily's attention was taken by the sight of the houses and her nausea began to subside a little. She was astounded by so many buildings together. Of course, she had seen pictures of crowded housing, but it was nothing like seeing the real thing. They seemed to go on for ever, row on row of them, all with their little gardens at the front, often with a vehicle parked on the driveway or in the road.

The traffic was especially frightening. Cars, trucks and buses appeared, moving at awesome speeds, coming towards her as if they meant to crash straight through the bus, then seeming to miss at the last moment, to disappear with amazing rapidity, somewhere behind her. Other vehicles overtook them. It was like a great dance of metal beasts, a weaving, wavering dance. Occasionally one blared, like a creature in pain, making her start like a panicked hare from her seat. Chris held on to to her, his soothing voice obviously attempting to calm her. A figure on a motorised bicycle roared by

131

the window looking like a demon god, its face a black reflecting mask.

Finally Chris said, 'Here, this stop will do. Let's get you into the fresh air.'

Immediately they were off the bus Emily was sick in the gutter.

Some passer-by said, 'Ugghhh, disgustin'. Been drinking', I'll bet.'

'No, we haven't!' called Chris, holding on to the bent-over Emily with his arm and glaring at the speaker. 'She's just not well.'

'You ought to get her a cup of tea or somethin' then. Poor love looks like death.'

Chris thought this was a good idea and steered the distressed Emily towards a tea stall.

To Emily, the streets were crowded with strangely dressed people, some with horrible faces. A group of youngsters began jeering at her, as she wiped the vestiges of vomit from the corners of her mouth with a lace handkerchief. This crowd of creatures had those amongst them with purple and green hair, shaved into a shape she recognised from an illustration of an Indian warrior in James Fenimore Cooper's novel *The Last of the Mohicans*. They had grotesque faces, full of pins. They wore ugly war paint and dressed in tattered clothes, with chains hanging from them. She could not tell who were the boys and who were the girls amongst them. They were carrying cans, which they put to their mouths every so often.

'Are they Red Indians?' asked Emily.

'Indians?' Chris repeated, then noticing the group, said, 'Naw, they're punks. Idiots. Take no notice of them. They're not really as hard as they look. It's the skinhead gangs you have to look out for.'

Chris was the fount of knowledge here. She was the helpless stranger. While it made him feel powerful, he also felt a great weight of responsibility. He was certain now that bringing her to the seafront was the wrong thing to do, and that he would be in trouble over it. He felt tender towards her too, and hated the thought that she was distressed. He mentally kicked himself for his stupidity.

'I'll get you a cup of tea to settle your stomach, then we'll go back again,' he told her. 'I'm sorry you're upset.'

Emily rallied. 'I'm a bit better now. I hate all these vehicles hurtling by. They frighten me. They sound so angry, like giant insects. Please take me home, Christopher.'

Chris stared at the cars and then said, 'They're only doing about thirty – there's a cop car just along there.'

This meant nothing to her whatsoever. She stared into a dark barn full of box-like machines from whence issued sounds she had never heard before: whistles, whizzes, bells, strange croaky voices repeating such phrases as ' . . . *you have killed seventeen aliens, congratulations, victorious earth warrior, you have killed eighteen aliens, you have killed . . .*' and music that hurt her ears with its discordant tones and high volume.

One machine, like a black squashed piano, was close to the doorway of the barn and she could see a boy playing on it. The screen had bright, flashing, garish colours that hurt her eyes, even from that distance. The boy looked frantic as his hands

133

jumped erratically from one knob to the other, as if his life depended upon the outcome of his manipulations. The machine kept *pinging* as shapes appeared and disappeared, running along moving pictures of walls and streets and houses, jungle and desert, changing, changing, changing.

There was a strong smell of sweat and over-cooked food in the atmosphere, especially at the entrance to the barn full of machines. Emily staggered away to escape from the putrid odours.

'I really – really would like to go home,' she mumbled.

She felt dizzy and would have fallen over if she hadn't grabbed hold of something.

'Don't faint on me now,' cried Chris in a horrified voice. 'Oh heck . . .'

Emily leaned against a portly statue wearing a blue coat and blue sailor's hat. She saw that it had a beak and resembled a duck-like creature. There was another statue on the other side of the great barn, looking a little like a giant mouse in clothes. Emily knew that certain heathen peoples used to have painted statues guarding their sacred buildings and wondered if the barn was some kind of pagan area of town where strange temples had been built, with guardian idols at the doorways, and inside the frenzied rituals of the worshippers.

Chris said, 'Mind your poncho thing on Donald Duck. He's a bit greasy.'

'It's all buildings and ugly lights and noise,' she said, staring down at a crack in the pavement, concentrating on this for a while in the hope of getting rid of her dizziness. 'Everywhere is just horrible. Horrible.'

134

The outside world was such a disappointment to her. She had left Rattan Island expecting to see machines, but the number and noise of them was quite overpowering. The people, too, were strange and frightening. They looked hostile and spoke so aggressively. Christopher, she knew, was doing his best for her now that he had realised his mistake in bringing her to this terrible place, and she was in his hands.

She didn't altogether blame Christopher for what was happening to her, but she hated her father's being right. It made her angry to think how he would gloat over her distress, if he knew what had occurred. It gave her some strength and resolve not to let the experience crush her desire to find out more about life in the modern world.

Christopher was not as perfect as she imagined he would be – he was no Sir Galahad – but he was nice and she was reluctant to think badly of him. If he managed to get her home safely, then she would forgive him for bringing her to this hell, and if he did not, nothing would matter anyway. She was sure she could not survive long in this place.

A further noise startled her at this moment, coming from the direction of what appeared to be an inn. Some drunks were staggering out on to the pavement, yelling loudly. Their harsh voices terrified Emily. A man wearing a blue woollen hat seemed to be fighting with a second man, who swung his arms and roared. The man in the hat laughed raucously, avoiding the blows, kicking out with his right foot occasionally.

Emily swallowed hard and looked. She was terribly afraid.

13

Chris was aware that the mid-afternoon drunks were beginning to spill out of the seafront pubs. After a tussle one of them threw an empty beer can into the road and yelled to his mate to get the car. The swear-words he used made Chris wince, but when he glanced at Emily he was pretty sure she had not understood any of it. She still looked very pale. He decided they ought to go back to Barling straight away, before something else happened to upset her.

A pop song was blaring out from the arcade: 'Highbrow Girl', by a new cult band. Chris wanted Emily to listen to it with him, because it was a song he liked very much, but she seemed to be overwhelmed by everything. She mumbled that she was drowning in a sea of noise, colour and confusion.

'Let's cross the road and walk along the beach a bit,' he said to her, gently taking her arm. 'There's not so much noise and stuff past the gasworks.'

She allowed herself to be guided across the road, once the traffic had stopped for them, but not without glancing fearfully at the cars the whole while. When they had reached the promenade, she shied away from the direction of the fairground with its spinning big wheel and the spider rocketing around at blinding speeds. Chris could see that the screams coming from that direction were disconcerting to her, and he hastened to assure her that they were screaming in fun.

'People like to be scared sometimes,' he told her. 'The big dipper's worse, but they don't run that in the winter. That's that upsy-downsy thing you can see, with rails on it. It's like – like an open-topped train, going up and down steep hills. You get some that go in a loop, so you get turned upside down.'

She shuddered. 'It doesn't sound like fun. It sounds as if they are concerned for their lives.'

'I know. They want it to sound like that. It's – it's part of the fun.'

'What is that terrible odour?' she asked him. 'It is that which is making me feel ill.'

He sniffed the air, unable to smell anything unusual, and then took a very intelligent guess. 'Car fumes, probably – and petrol. It'll get blown away on the beach.'

'Candy floss, love?' said a fat woman at a stall they passed on crossing the promenade. 'Ice cream?'

'No thanks,' replied Chris. 'Bit cold for ice creams.'

'What about a nice beefburger or hotdog then?'

'Dog?' gasped Emily. 'She's selling cooked dog meat?'

'Sausage,' Chris corrected her. 'It's nothing to do with dogs. I dunno why they call it that.'

'You want one?' insisted the woman.

'No thanks,' said Chris again.

The woman sniffed. 'Suit yourself.'

Two young boys on skateboards almost ran them down.

137

'Watch it!' cried Chris.

'Watch it yerself, ratface,' yelled one of them over his shoulder.

Chris glared at the boys, wondering whether to chase after them, then decided he ought to stay with Emily. On the road beside the strand six motorcycles hammered by with thunderous roars making Emily stumble backwards. He felt it was time to get her on the beach.

They made the shingled foreshore without further mishap. He ran with her down to the water, where it was relatively quiet. A dune of sand and pebbles separated them from the bustle of the seafront now. Emily announced that the smell from the sea was doing her good. She breathed in deeply, several times. Chris asked her if she would like to rest on one of the patches of sand for a while and she said she would. They sat together watching the waves ripple in over the estuary mouth. The longest pleasure pier in the world stretched out like a straight black arm over the water and Kent was visible in the distance, a misty far-off land. Chris pointed to a giant chimney on an island out in the estuary. A tall flame of waste gas burned from its top, making it appear like a huge candle.

'That's a cat-cracker,' he told Emily knowledgably. Then he added, grinning, 'Nothing to do with cats.'

She managed a weak smile at his attempt at humour.

'Tide's in,' Chris remarked.

'Yes, it is, isn't it? Look at that seagull, perched on that post over there. He looks like he's waiting for someone, doesn't he? Perhaps a friend from over the Channel?'

'They're noisy devils, aren't they?' Chris said. 'Seagulls. All that carking. They get on our roof and wake me up in the mornings. Between them and the pigeons it's a wonder I get any sleep at all.'

She laughed at this. 'You should see them out in the fields, following the plough. They're like an angry mob. I don't think I like seagulls very much, do you?'

It was the first time they had communicated properly with each other and Chris realised it was because they were talking about natural things. Behind them, just twenty metres away, were scenes which she did not understand, just as he had difficulty in understanding her home life. Yet beyond both of these enclosed worlds was a greater world, some of which both of them understood, some of which was still waiting for both of them to discover. They knew they were attracted to each other because of their differences – they found each other exotic and exciting – but they had common ground too in that they both felt outsiders in their own enclosed worlds: Chris because he was living with a single parent in an isolated village, and Emily because she wished to break away from her prison.

'D'you dance at all?' he asked her.

'Dancing?' She turned to look at him and he was gratified to see her eyes sparkling. 'Oh, I love to waltz.'

'Well, I don't waltz much,' he admitted, 'but I'm a pretty good disco dancer . . . ah, er, disco's sort of free movement and such. You do what you like, but you've still got to keep the rhythm. I don't like to brag but you should see me move. Like *Saturday Night Fever.* Kids are pretty envious of me sometimes. Disco – it's a lot faster than ballroom stuff.'

'Ballroom?'

'Well, all that stuff – waltzing and foxtrot.'

'I don't know anything about foxtrotting,' she confessed, 'but I'd love to see you dance the disco sometimes.' She gave him a gummy smile which quickened his heartbeat.

'Oh, right, well, I will, sometime. Hey look, there's a Thames barge . . .'

Ships were passing in and out of the estuary mouth, mostly small cruise liners and tankers, but closer to the shore a rusty-red-sailed boat with a dark hull was cutting through the waters. It was a touch of yesteryear, one of the Thames barges that had in the last century been used to carry goods up and down the river, but were now mainly showpieces.

'Oh, I've seen pictures of those,' cried Emily, clapping her hands together. 'Isn't it *delightful.* It looks like a wounded butterfly skipping over the water.'

Chris stood up and began skimming stones over the surface of the sea, until a fisherman glared at him.

'Shall we walk on a bit, now?' he said. 'You ought to be getting back.'

They walked along the beach, not saying anything now, until they reached the jetty opposite the gasworks. There they waited for the bus, with Emily becoming more anxious about the journey by the minute. Chris did not see any other way of getting her back to the farm in time though.

'It mightn't be so bad this time,' he told her. 'Maybe it was just because it was your first time?'

But Emily felt just as unwell on the way home and when they reached the little row of cottages at the end of the Barling road, she was again ill. However, she admitted she was relieved to be back again and confessed that, though the trip had been a nightmare for her, she had found it interesting, 'with much to think about' and she added, 'I have enjoyed your company greatly, Christopher. Despite our vastly different backgrounds we seem to get on well together, don't you think?'

'You didn't hate it then – all of it?'

'Not you,' she added. 'You were very kind, Christopher. You just did not understand how little I know of the outside world and you cannot be blamed for that.'

'I should never have made you go on the bus.'

'You were not to know I would be ill. Anyway,' she smiled bravely, 'it's over now. We are home. Oh dear,' she glanced towards the direction of the farm, 'I do hope dear Anne hasn't been waiting all this time. She will have become dreadfully cold and she's never *quite* well, you know. I should hate her to catch a chill.'

They walked back along the top of the dyke, with the winds fingering the grasses at their feet, and the winter birds peppering the skies. It was the time of the year when flocks of knots suddenly rose like buckshot out of the salt marshes and played follow-my-leader over the landscape.

Black columns of cumulus were growing ominously on the eastern horizon and Chris wondered whether he would manage to reach home without getting wet.

As they approached the ford a figure on the landscape suddenly moved, running down the cockleshell track from the direction of the farm towards Rattan Creek and clasping a shotgun. There was a deadly intent in the way the figure moved. It filled Chris with dread. The wind was lifting the grey-black hair wildly and its coat flapped after it like the wings of a supernatural fiend. Had a diabolic scarecrow suddenly detached itself from the clay and come charging down on them, Chris would not have been more surprised and astonished – or more frightened.

Whoever it was had obviously been standing on a knoll, watching the sea wall, waiting for the pair of them to return.

Emily stopped and gasped.

'Papa!' she cried. 'They must have come home early. He's *very* angry. Run, Christopher, run!'

Chris saw the enraged man coming down towards them at a rapid pace and he agonised for a moment. Should he leave Emily to face this father alone, or should he stay and try to explain that it was all his fault that his daughter was late home? What was the big deal anyway, they had only been to Southend. But the tone in Emily's voice, and the face of the oncoming man, told Chris that there would be no time for explanations. If he stayed, he would be sure to be thrashed, perhaps worse.

'OK, 'bye, Emma,' he said, 'see you later,' and took to his heels, racing along the road towards Barling.

There was no point in staying to try to reason

with the enraged man. Especially when Craster was carrying a deadly weapon. Emily's father was surely not going to hurt his own daughter? Chris knew it was *his* blood the farmer was after and by remaining behind and trying to make explanations Chris would only make the situation worse.

But would the farmer follow him?

PART FOUR:

A Thing Most Brutish

14

He looked back once, to see Emily's father take a passing swipe at his daughter with his left hand. Emily's arms were up, shielding her head, and the blow caught her across the shoulders. Then her father swore at her and continued on after Chris. Any hopes that the man would be satisfied with getting his daughter back in one piece were soon dispelled. He wanted Chris's blood, very badly.

If he had not been scared enough before, Chris was terrified now. The man looked as if he wanted to kill him. Chris cut away from the road, into the fields, running towards a distant farm. His legs were trembling as he ran, but he knew that if he fell he would probably not get up again. His chest heaved and his breath hurt his throat. His terror gave power to his running and not for one second did he consider stopping.

When he looked back next, the man was only fifty metres behind him and Chris sobbed out, 'You touch me and my dad'll take you to court – '

The only effect this had on Chris's pursuer was to elicit a yell of rage from him. Then, miraculously, Emily's father tripped in a furrow and fell heavily to the ground. The shotgun flew from his grasp, somersaulted, and hit the brick-hard ground, exploding on impact. The shot blasted a sod of earth to pieces not a half-metre away from the farmer's own head.

Shaken by the sudden noise, which had rooks flying up in confusion from a nearby spinney, Chris almost fell down himself.

Chris then got his second wind and flew over the rutted ground, putting distance between him and the man.

Emily's father was quickly back on his feet, but by that time Chris was two hundred metres ahead. When Chris dared to look behind again, he saw that the man had slowed to a stop and was clutching his side, a sure sign of the stitch. The cold sweat of relief came over Chris and he began sobbing again, knowing he had escaped a severe beating. He began to be angry at the man now, for chasing him and frightening him so badly.

'All because of a little trip out,' cried Chris, loudly. 'We didn't do anything wrong. You wait, I'll get the law on to you. You can't go around chasing people with guns.'

Gradually, Chris slowed to a walk. He reached the next farm and found a track on the other side. This he followed alongside the river wall. He kept clear of the main road, for fear that Emily's father might go back to his farm and get a car or something, to chase after him. Finally he reached the edge of Rochford, where he caught a bus for Paglesham Eastend.

When he got off the bus the skies were black and it was pouring with rain: a cold, hard, sleety rain. He put up the collar of his leather jacket and did his best to keep himself dry over the last two hundred metres. Finally, he was at his own door and entered his house, thankful to be home.

Tom was there.

'Hello, drowned rat,' Tom said, smiling.

Sally said, 'Oh, Chris. Go and get changed quickly, you'll catch cold.'

Chris went up to his room and when he had changed he was so exhausted he lay down on his bed and fell asleep. The sound of a taxi drawing up outside woke him. Chris looked through the bedroom window, electrified as he saw Emily's father get out and stride down the path. Obviously Emily had told her father his address and he was here to extract retribution.

There was a hammering on the door, some loud voices, then Sally called up the stairs, 'Chris, come down here, please!'

He descended the stairs slowly, his heart pounding.

Emily's father was saying, '. . . I want the boy thrashed.'

'You what?' said Sally. 'I'm sorry, Mr Craster, that sort of thing isn't on the agenda in this household, now or at any time.'

Tom said quietly, 'Let's hear what he's done before Mrs Hatchly decides whether any punishment's necessary, shall we?'

Chris reached the bottom of the stairs just as Emily's father, dripping water from his coat and broad-brimmed hat, was waving a fist in Tom's face snarling, 'Listen, you, your son abducted my daughter and if I get my hands on him I'll thrash him myself. Little toads like him understand only one thing – a good hiding – a thorough whipping.

149

The girl's taken her punishment, now let him take it like a man.'

'By God, you won't hurt my boy, whatever he's done,' shouted Sally. 'Tom, go and phone for the police. The man's a maniac.'

Craster used a string of foul words which made even Tom blink with surprise.

Tom stood directly in front of the raging, soaked Craster and said just as quietly as before, 'Watch your language, man, this is someone's home. Now, he's not my son. I happen to be a friend of the family ...'

A light gleamed in Craster's eyes. 'Oh, *that* kind of arrangement, is it? No wonder the boy's the way he is. My girls have been brought up to observe decent behaviour – respect for parents and *family* life – and they've had good models in their mother and myself. Then someone like your guttersnipe boy comes along and corrupts them.'

Tom's face went hard. 'I told you, he's not my boy. I wish he was. I don't know what you mean by "that kind of arrangement", Mr Craster, but we'll let that pass for the moment. One thing I can assure you – there'll be no violence, understand? I'm a social worker. One finger on that boy and you'll find yourself in court, and I'll make sure you go to prison. Now, unless you calm down I'll do as Mrs Hatchly said, I'll get the police.'

Veins stood out on Craster's brow. His wet cheeks were taut across the bones and his lips were thin purple lines. There was a drop of white spittle in the corner of his mouth, like a fleck of foam.

Chris could see the farmer's hands curling and uncurling, as if he was longing to hit the man in

150

front of him. Finally he spluttered, 'That boy abducted my daughter. I'd say that was worthy of a prison sentence too, wouldn't you?'

Sally went a little pale at this and shot a glance at Chris.

'How old is your daughter, Mr Craster?' she asked, in a fearful voice.

'Almost fifteen . . .' fumed the farmer, but if he was going to add anything to these two words, he did not get the chance, because Sally exploded in derisive laughter.

'*Fifteen?* You're accusing one fifteen-year-old of abducting another?'

Tom turned to Chris and asked, 'Did you force this girl to go with you in any way?'

Chris struggled to get out the words. The atmosphere was so thick with emotion he was beginning to think he might have committed the equivalent of murder. Finally he managed to blurt out, 'No, course not. Emily sent me that letter you saw, Mum. She asked me to meet her – go for a walk. That's all. I can prove it, I've still got the letter.'

This statement seemed to do little to calm the irate Craster, who pointed a finger over Tom's shoulder. 'You took her to Southend, you little toad.'

Tom said, 'Hey, hey, let's have less of the name-calling. Now unless you calm down – and I mean it this time – I shall close this door in your face and call someone.'

Chris cried, 'We didn't mean to go to Southend – at least, not in the beginning – I thought she'd like a bus ride. Emily's never been off Rattan Island, Mum. She's like a prisoner. He keeps her there –

and her sisters. They don't know anything about the real world outside. She went all funny when we got off the bus. She didn't know what was going on. It made her giddy. That wasn't my fault – it's *his*. He keeps them on the farm – that's what Emily told me.'

Tom's face hardened. 'Is this true?' he asked Craster.

Craster's expression underwent a change now.

Inside he was beginning to regret letting his anger get the better of him. This man in front of him was a member of the social services. Here was someone who could gain a court authority to investigate life at the farm, if he could convince a magistrate that the Craster children were at risk in some way. Though Craster believed there was little that could be discovered which could be used against him, he knew his views on child-rearing might attract attention from the psychologists and social workers – perhaps even hated television and newspapers. His whole way of life might be presented out of context and he did not relish the invasion of his privacy.

Though his manner was no more conciliatory than before, he adopted a dignified posture. 'It's true,' he explained, in a more controlled tone of voice, 'that my daughters don't meet many outsiders. We've raised them according to older and I believe *better* traditions, more wholesome values, from a time when decent and moral behaviour was considered admirable. My wife and I do not approve of the decadence and ugliness into which the world of today has sunk. For my part, I think technology has been responsible for the decline in

152

ethical behaviour and I intend to keep my daughters from coming into contact with the devices you people worship – cars, computers, and the like. Our pleasures on the farm are simple – books, music, poetry – and I don't believe it's wrong to protect our children from the lawlessness and perversions of the modern world, with its drugs, criminals, rapists – and the likes of that degenerate boy you have there.'

Sally said, 'My son is *not* degenerate. He's as decent and wholesome as your own children. All he did was what any normal boy does – he went out on a date with a girl ... did you touch her?' she asked Chris.

'I held her hand. We didn't even kiss,' mumbled Chris, embarrassed.

She turned to Craster again. 'Did your daughter say my son touched her?'

'I don't think that's the point.'

'Of course it's the point. The point is, what have they done wrong? As far as I can see,' Sally said, 'they didn't do a damn thing wrong. They were just two young kids out enjoying "simple pleasures". A ride on a bus! My God,' she put her arm around Chris, 'I think that's *beautiful*. You talk about ugliness and old values. What could be more innocent than a boy and girl going for a ride on a bus? Just get out of here, Mr Craster, and don't come back.'

'You keep him away from my daughter, or I'll give him something he won't forget,' warned the farmer. Then he stalked off down to the path and along the track.

Tom closed the door. 'Well, he's gone. What a terrible man.'

Sally muttered, 'Jack would have punched him on the nose for some of the things he said.'

Tom stopped and stared at her. 'And you think that's what I should have done? It would have improved the situation, wouldn't it, resorting to a brawl on your doorstep? I don't have the same rights as Jack, in any case . . .'

'No, you're right, Tom, you don't. Jack is Chris's father.'

Tom gave her an ironic smile. 'And I'm just the guy who comes here occasionally to see you?'

She shrugged, folding her arms. 'Well, it's true, isn't it? All right, it would have worsened the situation if you had hit him, but *I* sure as hell felt like it. Jack would have flattened him in an instant. It wouldn't have done any good, but I would have felt better about it. That *man*,' she seethed, 'calling Chris those names as if he was entitled to. I should have spat in his eye.'

'But you didn't,' said Tom, 'because you know that would have been the wrong thing to do.'

'I'm fed up with doing the right thing and letting people like that walk all over me.'

'I don't think he walked all over you. I think you stood your ground with dignity and showed him up for what he is – a boorish, deluded man. I think you handled it magnificently – and,' Tom added, 'so did I, so did we all. Chris could have stayed upstairs – Craster was enough to frighten anyone – but he didn't. He came down and defended himself well. You can look on that as a defeat if you like. I think it's a complete victory and I'm sorry you don't see it that way.'

Chris said, 'I agree with Tom.'

'You would,' flashed Sally at him. 'And this is your fault, Chris. What in heaven's name are you doing, taking out a girl who doesn't know her head from her heels? You ought to have more sense.'

Chris could see that she was overwrought and was probably saying things simply in order to release some of her pent-up feelings, but he had had enough for one day.

'You're rotten sometimes, Mum,' he said, quietly, and went back upstairs to his room. He flung himself on his bed, disgusted with Sally and all the other adults in his life.

He could hear Sally weeping downstairs, and Tom trying to comfort, but he couldn't go down. He was fed up with the whole business. Outside the rain was hitting the window-panes with considerable force. Chris stared moodily out at this gloomy aspect. For all he cared it could rain for ever.

While he lay there he thought about the shotgun. He had said nothing about it downstairs because he knew it would cause an almighty row. Chris had had enough of rows for one day and also he didn't want Emily's father to be in trouble with the police because of him. If that happened Emily might not *ever* want to see him again, while at the moment things were bad but could improve. Nothing serious enough to keep them apart for ever had occurred.

Chris lay on his bed staring at the ceiling and thinking of Emily. He went through the afternoon in detail in his head, thinking how brave she had been, on several counts. First of all she had met with him when her father strongly disapproved of her meeting with boys. If he was the first boy she had ever been out with, then she had risked it for *him*, but never for any other boy. That was worth a million in his estimation.

Secondly, and more importantly, she had been courageous in facing a world which clearly terrified her. A world that had bewildered her and made her physically sick. A lot of the girls he knew would have had a screaming fit, had they been put under a similar amount of stress. Not Emily, though. She had taken it badly, but quietly, and when she had recovered she hadn't turned around and blamed him for the whole mess.

He *had* to see her again, even if it killed him.

15

'Lord forgive our daughter for her terrible sin . . .'

James, Hannah, Charlotte and Ann Craster were standing in the shape of a horseshoe in the parlour, dressed in their dark Sunday clothes, prayer books in their right hands. The two girls were pale and upset. Their mother looked tearful, with dark circles around her eyes and hands that held not only her book, but a lace handkerchief, which she continually twisted around the fingers of her left hand. James Craster had pinched lips, an austere expression, and stood pole-stiff.

Kneeling in the centre of the horseshoe gap, head bowed as if about to be beheaded by an executioner, was Emily. This Sunday, today, the service was for her. They had to try to scourge her of her wrongdoing, to bring her back into the heart of the family, where they were waiting to welcome her – if she was truly penitent.

Emily's father had told her earlier, there could be no forgiveness without contrition on her part. It was necessary that she recognised her failing. She had been wrong, entirely wrong, to go off without permission into the outside world, the very place from which her parents were trying to protect her.

'But if I had asked,' Emily said reasonably, 'you would not have let me go.'

'Of course not,' thundered her father, his nose a few centimetres away from hers, 'it's unthinkable. I have spent my life trying to keep you from boys like that.'

'Boys like what?' she asked.

'Boys who wish to exploit your innocence!' her father yelled, somewhat enigmatically. 'Your purity! I want to know how you came to meet this boy.'

'Serendipity, papa,' said Emily, sweetly.

He struck her across the face.

Hannah Craster was not present at this interrogation, having been despatched on an errand by her husband. He knew she would not approve of his methods of discipline and he intended to get the whole thing over with before Hannah returned. In his opinion Emily had to be taught a lesson she would not forget until the day she died. He *had* to protect her from the evil of young men and if it took pain to instill her with fear of reprisals, then he had to administer that pain, even though the last thing he wanted to do was hurt one of his daughters.

'Don't get insolent with me, you little trollop. Now, how did he know to come here? I want the truth.'

Emily sobbed. 'I just *saw* him, walking on the dyke, that's all. I was just out strolling with Anne, getting some fresh air, Papa . . .'

'How did he know to come here?'

'He – he said he saw us once when he crossed the marshes – they were frozen over and he crossed them. He looked in at the window and saw us all.'

This seemed to satisfy her father. 'That footprint!' he nodded as if a question had been answered. 'The boy's a predator. If he comes here again, I'll fill his backside full of buckshot – *then* we'll see if he wants to prey on my daughters. Just let me catch him trespassing on my land and we'll settle accounts then.

'Now, you, Emily, must take your punishment. I have a mind to lock you in the cellar for the day . . .'

Dread coursed through Emily's heart. The cellar was the pit of hell: all the terrors of humankind, all the tortures, the nightmares, the manifestations of demons and ghouls, were down in that cellar. To be locked in the cellar for one single hour would have sent Emily mad. The devil was down there in the form of a large black beast, with a long scaly tail, small evil eyes, and fat body – and *teeth* – two rows of sharp needle teeth.

'Papa, *please*,' she shrieked, frantically clawing at his waistcoat. 'Not the cellar, please. Have pity, Papa.'

This display of almost lunatic fear frightened even James Craster. He peeled her fingers from his waistcoat in revulsion, while staring down into the wild eyes buried in a face contorted with terror. It was true he wanted to punish her badly for her offence, but he did not want a daughter gibbering on the edge of madness at the end of the day. Yet what was he to do, to impress his will upon this wayward child?

He made a decision and gave her a choice. 'It must be the cellar – or a sound thrashing!' he said.

Emily bit her lip and said, 'Thrashing, Papa.'

He nodded, grimly, and took a leather belt from the top of his desk where he had placed it earlier.

'Turn around and grip the edge of the desk,' he ordered his daughter. 'The belt never did me any lasting harm, but it did make me think before doing wrong twice. This will be both a punishment and hopefully a deterrent, child.'

When he could see that her grey cotton dress was stretched tautly across her back, he lashed her three times in quick succession, not as hard as he had once been thrashed himself by a zealous schoolmaster forty years before, but hard enough to make Emily shriek in pain.

He almost put the belt down after those three strokes, worried and upset by her cries, but he was desperate for obedience and he knew Emily would not give him that obedience if her punishment was not severe.

While she sobbed, he struck her three more times, harder still.

His breath was coming out fast and stale, as he said in a choked voice, 'You brought it on yourself, child.'

At that moment the door flew open and Hannah stood there, with Anne and Charlotte behind her. Hannah stared at the weeping Emily, lying in a heap on the floor at the base of the desk, then at her husband holding the belt. Hannah went to her child and hugged her to her breast.

'Oh, my poor Emily,' she whispered, feeling the damp blood soaking through the girl's dress.

She turned to look up at her stone-faced husband with contempt.

'You stupid man,' she said. 'You utter fool. I hope you . . .'

Hannah's anger at her husband dissipated a little once she obtained from him a promise that he would never hit any of the girls again. She had to make James realise that violence was not the answer to disobedience, disappointing as that defiance of their wishes had been.

James Craster himself had calmed somewhat, since then, but he was no less disappointed in Emily. Now at this special service he intoned: 'Remember the fifth commandment, daughter. Honour thy father and thy mother,' holding up the Book of Common Prayer as if he were offering it to some unseen figure in the rafters. 'Honour thy father and thy mother! Now let us pray. We humbly beseech thee, O Father, mercifully to look upon our infirmities . . .'

Next they sang an appropriate hymn to the tune of 'Au Clair de la Lune':

> Walking in the garden,
> at the close of day
> Adam tried to hide him
> when he heard God say:
> 'Why are you so frightened,
> why are you afraid?
> You have brought the winter in,
> made the flowers fade.'

When the service was finished, James Craster slammed his book shut and said, 'Now, child, are you sorry for what you have done?'

161

Emily said in a soft voice, 'I haven't done anything.'

James Craster's face twisted in anger. 'You disobeyed *me*, you disobeyed your *mother* – what have we been talking about here? Obedience to one's parents. You are a child. You need the guidance of your elders. Why are you so stubborn? Say you are sorry and we shall forgive you.'

Emily was silent for a long while, then she said quietly, 'I'm sorry, Father.'

'What?' he bellowed. 'We can't hear you.'

Emily looked up and said fiercely. 'You don't want me to say I'm sorry – you want to *humiliate* me in front of my sisters. Stop it! I won't have it, do you hear. I won't have it.'

Both Charlotte and Anne were looking with wide eyes, first at Emily and then at their father, watching this battle of wills with awe. They were used to their father being angry over something but his wrath was usually reserved for those outside the farm, or farm workers who did not meet his standards, or even animals who failed him in some way. He had been very annoyed with one or other of the girls in the past, but never so furious that he could not control himself. Today was different.

Emily's reaction, though no stranger to them, was stronger than they had previously witnessed. She had always been the wilful one. If Anne did not like a piece of gristle on her dinner plate, she would scrape it into the fire when her mother was not looking. Charlotte would eat it, though it made her retch. Emily, however, would sit with it on her plate, though her mother would tell her she *must* finish her meal before she would be allowed to leave the table. Emily would be there when nightfall came, followed by daybreak, until finally Mother would give in and let her down from the table.

James Craster cried, '*You* won't have it, by God . . .?'

Hannah interrupted with, 'I think the child has apologised, James. Let's leave it be. Go to your room, Emily. Your punishment isn't over yet. You must stay there for the whole of Sunday while we enjoy our day. You may not have lunch, but I shall send you some dinner later. We're still very displeased with you – but nothing more will be said on the subject.'

Emily climbed the stairs to her room with her emotions bubbling like a froth in her breast. There was anger there, and guilt, and frustration, and love and hate. She understood why they were upset with her, but she did not agree with her father's methods of dealing with it. She did not mind being beaten, but she would not be humiliated! He was trying to make her into a pathetic creature, afraid of him and afraid of the world, and she would not submit to that kind of treatment. He had always wanted them to be like the Brontë sisters, and Emily Brontë was not a piteous woman.

Once she was in her room, however, Emily burst into tears. She lay on her bed and sobbed into the pillow until it was quite wet. Then, with the tears over once again, she stared out of the window over the marshes of Paglesham, wondering whether Chris had been as unfortunate as her. She knew her father had been to Chris's house, but she did not know the outcome of that visit. All she knew was that when he returned James Craster was in a foul mood and the rest of the family suffered for it.

Charlotte came to see Emily and held her sister's hand, suffering with her.

'Oh, Em, we shouldn't have done it. It was very wrong of us. Papa should have beaten me, not you. I'm the eldest. I'm the one to blame.'

'Fiddlesticks,' cried Emily, irritated for once by her sister's search for contrition. 'I'm the one who met with Christopher – and I'm *glad*. I'm glad Papa beat me. I'd do it all again.' She burst into tears and sobbed into her pillow.

Charlotte was devastated. 'Oh, Lord, please don't, Em. It's bad enough having Mother weeping all the time. I think she cries for us, though . . .'

'And I'm crying for *me*, is that it? Well, I don't care. My back hurts. I'm allowed to cry if my back hurts, aren't I? And Papa keeps *criticising* me. I can cry over that too, I suppose? Oh, Charlotte, you're so silly sometimes.'

Charlotte stroked her sister's cheek, trying to share her pain. 'Papa shouldn't have beaten you, Em, even though you were quite wrong to run away. I think he'll see that, one day. But we must all try to get on with one another here. We're all so close, you know? I love you, Em.'

'Oh, you love everybody,' murmured Emily, a little ungratefully.

Charlotte smiled. 'Yes, but I love Mama, you and Anne best.'

'And Papa?'

'I – I love him too, of course.'

'And Chervil the pony?' asked Emily, a little wickedly.

Charlotte laughed. 'All right, everybody. I do love everybody. *Now* are you satisfied?'

Later in the day, Anne came to visit her. Anne, Emily realised, was very impressed by what she had done. To travel to Southend in a bus! Emily's father had expressly forbidden the girls to talk about her escape. He had told Emily he would be even more angry if she regaled her sisters with 'romantic nonsense' about life beyond the farm.

These warnings to her sisters did nothing to quash their curiosity, but in fact inflamed it.

'What was it like?' said Anne. 'Did you meet lots of people?'

Emily said, 'You know you're not supposed to ask.'

'It can be a secret between the two of us. No one else need know, dear Em. *Please* tell me.'

Emily rolled on to her side and stared at the wall.

'It was both hateful – and wonderful. I don't know. I became ill, with travelling on the bus, Anne. There was a woman,' she sat up abruptly, 'who wore a fur coat and nothing on underneath.'

'*Nothing?*' squeaked Anne.

'Well, practically nothing. She had on some kind of tight, black, silky pyjamas – nothing else. You could see her bosoms poking out of the top.'

Anne's eyes went wide and round, as impressed by Emily using that word as well as by the image the sentence produced. 'You couldn't?'

'Yes, really. And she was wearing shoes with heels like little stilts. When she sat down I thought her pyjamas would split, they were *so* tight. And her hair was cut as short as a man's – blonde and jaggedy. You should see the rouge and powder she

165

wore. There were girls as old as me with brightly coloured lips, orange cheeks, and brown and blue around their eyes, and their eyebrows like thin lines, and silver on their faces – real painted ladies from the theatre, except I'm certain they weren't, they were just ordinary girls like us.

'Some of them smelled horribly sweet though, as if they'd been bathing in perfume. A few of them looked *awful* as well. They had black or dark purple lips, masses of black around their eyes, white faces. They looked like corpses. I saw all those things Papa warned us about. There were girls in trousers, girls in all *sorts* of things . . .'

'And the boys?' said Anne, hopefully.

Emily frowned and shook her head. 'They wore peculiar clothes. Like Christopher. Did you see how peculiarly he was dressed, with that cap and leather jacket? I wanted to laugh at first, but most of the boys of his age dressed like that. Some boys wore paint on their faces too!'

'Really?'

'Yes, really. And they had hair fashions like American Red Indians, or often very long hair. I liked Christopher's hair,' said Emily dreamily. 'It was sort of longish and floppy, with a parting down the middle. I only saw it once because he wore that silly hat most of the time. He's very nice, isn't he? He treated me as if I were a lady.'

Anne was still struggling with the general scene and was not really interested in 'Emily's Christopher'.

'Short hair for the girls, long hair for the boys?'

'Yes, often,' confirmed Emily. 'There's been a sort of change around, in the twentieth century. Boys are more like girls and vice versa. Papa's right about one thing – the world out there *is* full of machines. Machines everywhere. I'm not sure I liked that part of it. They smelled so. There were motor vehicles everywhere, and fun-fair machines, some you would never believe – and such colours too. There was one stall open with ice cream to eat, and pink cotton wool called *candy fluss* or something, even though it was bitterly cold.'

'Did you taste some ice cream?' asked Anne quickly.

'No, I was too ill. Besides, the place where it was sold smelled of cooked meat.'

'I shouldn't care about the cooked-meat smell,' Anne said, seriously. 'I should still like to taste ice cream.'

Emily recalled how sick she had been and shook her head. 'You would not have liked it if you felt as I did. The place was horrible. The roads were greasy and dirty . . . ouch.' Emily had rolled on to her side, on to the shoulder where her father's belt had cut into her skin. The weals still hurt where he had administered the strap.

'Oh,' winced Anne, 'does it hurt, dear Em? Is it terribly painful?'

'Yes,' said Emily, through gritted teeth. 'It hurts.'

'Papa has never hit any of us before. He must be dreadfully angry with you, Em.'

'He has never hit any of us before now,' said Emily, staring hard at the window, 'and he'll never hit *me* again.'

In the evening Emily was allowed to go downstairs to dinner, but there was little said at the table.

The following morning she slipped out of the house and found Dan feeding the pigs. He looked wary as she approached.

'I been hearin' things about you, Miss,' he said. 'You run off on Saturday with some boy. No doubt it was the same one I took the letter to. Well, I can't take no more.'

'Don't worry, Daniel,' she said. 'I haven't come to ask any favours. I just wanted you to know that Papa doesn't know how Christopher received the letter. I didn't tell him about it, even though he strapped me.'

Dan stared at her. 'What d'you mean, he *strapped* you?'

'He beat me with his belt. Papa said I could be locked in the cellar for a day, or take the strap. So of course I chose to have the strap, for there's a big black rat in the cellar, you know, and he frightens me more than a little pain.'

She showed Dan a weal on the back of her hand, where she had put up her arms to defend herself and had caught the edge of James Craster's leather belt there.

Dan's eyes opened a little. 'Beat you? Did he now? I've a feelin' that's not quite legal in this day and age. No one cares about a slap or two, I shouldn't think, but to beat a child of your age – well, of any age . . .'

'Surely fathers are allowed to discipline their children?' said Emily, standing up for her papa. 'If they weren't they would lose respect as head of the household, wouldn't they?'

Although the fire of rebellion had not been quashed in Emily, and she thought her father wrong

168

for thrashing her, she would not hear criticism of him from outside the family.

'I don't think they are allowed, miss – not as bad as that there on your hand. Not according to what I've seen on a documentary. That's called child abuse, that is.'

'Well, anyway, Daniel, it's over and done with now. I just wanted you to know our secret is safe.'

'Well, I appreciate that, but I can't do it no more. I don't want to be held responsible for him going off into one of his blue fits and hurting people.'

Emily went back indoors before she was missed. She was supposed to be blacking the kitchen range: not a punishment but one of her usual chores. Charlotte was waiting for her just inside the kitchen door.

'What were you saying to Daniel Selby, Emily?' asked Charlotte in a strained voice.

'It's a secret between the two of us,' replied Emily.

Charlotte took her sister's two hands in her own and looked fearfully into her eyes.

'Em, please don't do anything naughty again. Papa is like an ogre at the moment. He's hardly human. It's wrong of you to enrage him so.'

'I wasn't going to,' said Emily, 'but Daniel Selby says Papa is not allowed to hit me as he did. It's against the law.'

'Emily, Papa *is* the law here.'

'Here, yes,' said Emily firmly, 'but not out there.'

16

Two days later a visitor arrived at the farm. James Craster was in the barn, harnessing the shire horses with Dan, when Charlotte came running from the house.

'Someone's come,' she said, a little breathlessly, 'from Southend Social Services Department.'

James Craster scowled. 'What the hell is this?' he grumbled. 'What's going on? We'll have the world and his wife at the farm soon. All right, I'll be there in a minute.'

Dan said, 'You go. I can take care of the harness.'

Dan Selby looked a little nervous. James Craster decided this was because his farm worker expected him to blow a fuse. Dan was right, though, it would not do to keep the visitor waiting.

He thought that if it was about the girls not going to school it would be best not to antagonise the man. Perhaps Southend Social Services were not in contact with the schools' people? James Craster knew that he was within his rights to educate his daughters at home and indeed had the blessing of the education authority.

'All right, Selby, I'll be back in a minute.'

James Craster marched over to the house to find, not a man but a woman, talking to his wife in their parlour. Charlotte had been sent away. The other two girls were in their rooms, doing their normal studies. James Craster thought he might take this woman up to see them afterwards, to show her how diligently his daughters worked. He might even encourage questions, to reveal their superior learning.

The stranger was thin – he judged her to be somewhere in her late twenties – wearing a trouser suit under a short, thick coat. Her features were pleasant enough and she was smiling, but he did not like the smile. It irritated him. So did her pony-tail hairstyle and her high, lace-up boots.

'What's going on?' he said, staring distastefully at the trouser suit.

Hannah was sitting on the sofa looking pale. She had her hands folded in her lap. She stared warningly at her husband.

'This lady has had reports that we're mistreating our children,' she told him.

James Craster's first instinct was to administer a blistering attack on people interfering with his life, but he wisely held his counsel. Instead he said, 'What kind of mistreatment?'

The woman said, 'My name is Joanne Stillman, Mr Craster. I'm a social worker.'

'So I understand.'

'Good.' She gave him another irritating smile. 'Now, my department has received a report that your daughter Emily has been physically punished for something – by you, Mr Craster. The report says you hit her with a leather belt and that she has severe bruises. I'm here either to confirm, or otherwise, that information.'

'Who told you this?' growled James Craster,

standing over her in his farming clothes, flat cap, and boots smelling of pig dung. 'It was that other social worker, wasn't it? That dolt at the boy's house? You people can't just march in here and disrupt our life. Who do you think you are? Get out of here. Where's your damn car?'

He couldn't remember having spoken about the belt to the man at the boy's house – he was regretting that his temper had run away with his tongue now – but he did recall talking about Emily having already received her punishment.

'My car is at the ford, but . . .'

'Then get down to it and leave us be.'

The smile had turned distinctly frosty. 'I can't do that, Mr Craster. I have my job to do. I have to tell you that the report we received was from an anonymous source, but I have to check on it. The possibility of child abuse is taken seriously under the Children's Act. You do have a daughter named Emily?'

'Yes,' said Hannah in a quiet voice.

'Could I see her, please?'

'No, you damn well can't,' snapped James Craster, infuriated by her persistence. 'I've told you – get off my property, or I'll have you thrown off.'

Instead of being alarmed by this threat, as he expected, Joanne Stillman stood up and looked directly into his face. 'Mr Craster, I don't think you realise what's going on here. If I leave the farm I shall come back with a police escort and a court order. Eventually, I *shall* see Emily. It would be much easier for everyone concerned if you co-operated with me on this.'

172

Hannah stood up. 'I'm going to fetch Emily,' she said.

'You'll do nothing of the sort,' cried James Craster.

'Don't bully me, James,' said Hannah, softly. 'You can't bluster out of this. We have to get it settled. I don't want my house full of policemen.'

Hannah was frightened of the consequences of what her husband had done. Even if *he* did not realise it, she certainly was aware that they might lose a daughter into the care of the social services, if it was not handled correctly from now on. James did not seem to understand that you could not whip your own child with impunity. There were laws against it.

Frustrations were building in Craster's breast as he saw no other way out for him. Surely he was entitled to discipline his own children? They could not tell him how to bring up his girls, could they? He knew he was out of touch with the outside world, but things had not changed that much, surely?

Emily was brought into the room looking a little puzzled. When questioned by the stranger lady, she looked first at her father, then at her mother, and then told the truth. Yes, her father had hit her. On request, she allowed the woman to see the top of her back. Only one or two of the half-dozen strokes had fallen there, but they were enough to tell Joanne Stillman that the child had undergone a severe beating. She turned to James Craster.

'You admit you did this?'

'The child did wrong. She'll tell you that herself,' he said. 'I punished her for running away. Any father would do the same. It's for her own protection. All sorts of terrible things can happen to her out there. It's the first time I've done it, but I'm not sorry. Now what are you damn well going to do about it, eh? Lock me up?'

She brushed past him, saying, 'That's not for me to decide. I only make recommendations.' She stopped in the doorway to the room. 'Mr Craster, Mrs Craster, I'm going to discuss this with my principal officer. I want to be sure you're not going to lay into Emily for this, or I'll have to find somewhere for her to go – a foster home. I expect there will be a case conference, which will involve the education authorities, the police, and your family doctor. You will be invited to attend too. You must take Emily to see your doctor today, to make sure there's no other injury. I'll be in touch with you shortly.'

With that Joanne Stillman left the house.

James Craster whirled on his daughter. 'This is your fault. If you hadn't run away . . .'

'I *didn't* run away, Papa, I simply went off the island for the afternoon. You're the one who punished me. Daniel Selby said it was illegal. He said you could get into trouble. It's *not* my fault, Papa, it's *yours.*'

He stepped forward, saying dangerously, '*Dan Selby?*'

Hannah cried, 'Leave her alone, James. You heard what the woman said. If you touch Emily again, she'll be taken away and put in a foster home. Be sensible, for heaven's sake.'

Though James Craster had no intention of striking his daughter again, he did want to confront

174

someone. He couldn't fight with women and girls, but he could get satisfaction elsewhere.

Dan Selby was leading one of the horses out of the barn when the farmer yelled at him from across the yard.

'Selby! You're getting too big for your boots!'

Dan stopped and stared. 'What's that?' he said.

James Craster strode up to him and stood in his path. 'Did you ring up the social services people and tell them I was beating my daughter?'

'No,' said Dan, 'I didn't.'

'You're a liar,' growled the farmer.

Dan let the reins to the shire horse drop, and said slowly and menacingly, 'You better take that back before you gets a thumpin', Mr Craster. You're older'n me, but I ain't standing for bein' called no liar, that's certain.'

Until now Craster had believed he had ultimate power over Dan Selby. Now his farm worker was threatening to strike him.

'You must have told on me,' he said. 'It wasn't that other social worker, because he never knew about the belt.'

Dan Selby stared narrow-eyed at his boss. 'It was no doubt my sister. She was shocked terrible when I told her about little Emily gettin' the strap. Maybe I shouldn't have told her, but I did, an' it's done now – so don't you go callin' me no liar, you hear?'

'I could sack you right now,' snarled Craster. 'You and your damned meddling.'

'You could, but you wouldn't get no one else up here to help you. You done too much sackin' in the past. An' let me tell you somethin' now, Mr Craster.

175

There's such a thing as Industrial Tribunals these days. You can't sack me unless you got good cause – otherwise you got to pay me compensation.'

'Have I, by God?' roared Craster.

At that moment Hannah came out of the house and walked over the frozen yard to the two men.

'Standing there arguing with the hired man won't help either, James,' said his wife. 'Dan, would you please hitch up the pony and trap and fetch Dr Stacey? Tell him we need him to look at Emily. He'll come.'

'Am I in employment or not?' Dan asked.

'Yes, of course you are. James, come to the house. We have to talk.'

Hannah was the one in command now. His role as the great patriarch and protector was a sham. The prickling sweat froze on his brow. There was a sharp pain developing between his eyes. He could not, he realised, challenge the forces of the state *and* retain the privacy he cherished so much. He felt helpless and at the mercy of others. The full impact and implications of what he had brought about by 'disciplining' his daughter washed over him in a cold wave.

As they crossed the yard, he trotted at her heels, saying, 'Hannah, what are we going to do . . .?'

'We must do as we're asked, if we're to keep the family together,' said Hannah. 'You must learn to keep your peace, James, even though you might be bursting to tell people where to go and what to do with their suggestions. This isn't a family matter which we can deal with ourselves. We have to prove to others we're responsible parents.'

Responsible parents? he thought with anguish.

176

*I've dedicated my whole life to being a responsible
parent.*

'You're right, Hannah, but it's hard. It's very,
very hard,' he said, miserably.

James Craster felt his world was crumbling
around him as he followed his wife back into the
house. His daughters were disobeying him, his
farm-hand was answering back and his wife was
handling him as if he were a child. What had he
done to deserve it? Was he not a God-fearing man,
who simply wanted the best for his family? Had he
not done everything for them, not caring for his
own needs and desires, but satisfying theirs first?
Hadn't they all been happy until Emily had stupidly
rebelled against his wishes and run away to
Southend with that boy?

When they were in the parlour, Hannah told him
that she was afraid that if they did not comply with
the authorities all their dreams would turn to dust.

'You should not have hit her, James, however
angry you were. It was a stupid act. Now we'll
have to fight tooth and nail to keep the girls here.'

'They won't take my daughters away from me?'
he cried, flinging his cap at her feet. 'They won't
do that, will they?'

'Well, you must make sure they *don't*, James,'
she replied with determination in her voice, 'not if
we do everything they say and promise it will not
happen again. But they may make us send the girls
to school . . .'

'Where they'll learn ugly habits, nasty ways,'
cried the anguished farmer. 'I've seen these girls
come out of school. They dress like tarts. They use
make-up. They wear their dresses up their back-

177

sides. They're foul-mouthed and ignorant. How is mixing with them going to help my lovely daughters, I ask you that, Hannah? How?'

'. . . which is why we've got to do everything in our power to seem helpful, reassuring and willing parents. Perhaps we can convince the social services people that we're good, responsible people and that you just lost your temper once – a single aberration which will never happen again – and that the girls are benefitting educationally from being at home. No doubt the representative from the education authority will be Edith, who's always been on our side in this, and she'll get us out of trouble. But we must keep our heads, do you understand, James?'

'I understand, woman. I'm not a damn child. And there's something I've been meaning to ask,' he added. 'Where were you when Emily met this boy the first time, that's what I'd like to know?'

Hannah stared her husband directly in the eyes. 'I was in the bathroom,' she said.

'In the bathroom? What were you doing in there? Not taking a bath in the middle of the day, that's for sure.'

'I was weeping.'

'Weeping?' he cried, in astonishment. 'Over what?'

Hannah Craster sighed. She wanted to explain to him about how she felt concerning the lack of love – real love – in their household, but then seeing the inflexibility in his eyes she knew it would be a useless exercise. 'A man like you,' she said, 'would not understand. Not in a million years.'

Upstairs, the three girls were together in Emily's room, hugging each other for comfort. Their father had raised his voice in the house before now, but never against their mother. The girls were frightened and upset. Emily kept crying because she imagined she had brought ruin upon the household, just as Branwell Brontë had brought ruin upon Haworth Parsonage.

Charlotte said, 'Don't cry, Em. It wasn't all your fault. Papa shouldn't have punished you as severely as he did, no matter what you did wrong. He knows that himself now. Papa – Papa does things without thinking sometimes.'

'But if I hadn't been bad, none of this would have happened,' cried Emily.

Anne surprised them by saying dramatically, 'Oh, yes, it would. It had to happen one day, you know. I shouldn't cry if I were you, Em. It was Fate who did it, not you.'

Some time later they heard the pony and trap coming up the cockleshell track and saw Dr Stacey with Dan Selby.

Soon their mother came up the stairs with Dr Stacey and shooed Charlotte and Anne back to their own rooms. Dr Stacey remained in Emily's bedroom with her mother. When he came out his face was like stone. The two sisters then rushed back to Emily's room, asking her what had been happening.

'The doctor examined my back,' Emily told them.

There were voices downstairs then, but too low for the girls to comprehend what was being said. Then Dan Selby helped Dr Stacey up into the trap below Emily's window and they could hear the doctor saying, 'Stupid man . . .'

179

PART FIVE:

O Brave New World

17

Chris was desperately in love. At first he had thought he never wanted to see Emily again, but those had been false feelings. He could not get her out of his mind, not for one minute. She just would not go away. Every film or television programme he watched, every record he heard, she was there, somewhere, in some form or another.

It was a hopeless love, doomed to wallow in music, long hours of dreaming and many walks along dykes, staring in the direction of her house, because he knew Mr Craster stood like Cerberus between them.

Emily was on his mind every waking minute. He lay on his bed for hours on end just picturing what she might be doing, going over and over their after- noon together, trying to find amongst the threads of remembered conversations little hints that she might return the love which threatened to over- whelm him. Her face was frustratingly fuzzy in his mind, and he wanted a clear picture, to adore. The only feature he could remember with any real clar- ity was the long black hair. He wished now he had taken a camera with him so that he would have her image to treasure, while he played *Highbrow Girl*.

Sally had got so sick of him playing it on their CD player that she had banned it. He copied it on to a tape and played it on his Walkman, walking around the house with earphones on and a face like damp rag. He found the aching feeling that never left him both enjoyable and horrible.

He wrote letters – endless letters. He tore them up and threw them away before he had signed them. Chris was a lost soul, wandering in the ether.

'For heaven's sake, snap out of it,' said Sally irritably. 'You're worse than a bear with a sore head.'

'I'm not grouchy,' he said, hurt. 'I just don't feel like talking, that's all. School's getting on my back again. You don't remember what it's like, being my age. Everybody wants to get at you.'

Sally was frying eggs for their breakfast, the pan spitting and snarling at her because she had the hob too high. Sally did not approve of fried breakfasts, but she knew her son did, and she was trying to lure him out of his cave of despondency into the real world again.

She turned to him and said, 'Well, here's one more thing to make you miserable – I'm thinking of getting back with your father.'

Chris looked at her disbelievingly. 'What do you want to do *that* for? I thought you hated him. You said you did.'

'I don't hate your father. At least, I do sometimes, but not the way you think. The line between love and hate is very thin, as you'll discover, my friend, before you're much older. He offered to get back together again the other day and the reason I'm considering it is not because I love or hate him, but for practical reasons.'

'What then?'

184

Sally sighed and hooked the fried egg out of the pan with a wooden spoon, unsuccessfully, breaking the yolk which dribbled all over her cooker. She let out a mild expletive, then answered his question. 'You – you're the reason. Ever since I divorced your father your schoolwork has gone to the dogs. And now you're getting into trouble outside school too, with this girl and her father. I can't cope with it all, Chris. I know teenagers are supposed to be difficult, but I never realised ... oh, I know you don't take drugs, or steal cars and joyride – in some respects you're a gem – but I want you to do well in life, son, and you were doing much better when Jack was with us.'

'That's rubbish,' he told her. 'I'm just going through a bad patch at school – and there's not much chance of seeing that girl again, is there? *He* keeps her locked up like some maiden in a castle tower.'

'Well, don't you get any thoughts of rescuing her. It's not our business. Tom says that a case worker from child protection is going round there now. This Mr Craster hasn't got away with it. They've caught up with him.'

'Why don't you marry Tom, instead?' grumbled Chris. 'He'd make a good father, I'm sure.'

Sally cocked her head to one side as she looked at her son. 'You're not impressed by Tom, either, don't kid me. Oh, yes, he's a nice man, a very nice man, and you're right, he probably would make a good father for you – but I've got to have some say in this. I'm not going to hitch myself to a man I'm only just *fond* of, for the rest of my life, just to get you over your teenage years, Christopher Hatchly.'

'You'd rather hitch yourself to a man who gets drunk and hits you, is that it?'

Sally was just raising a piece of egg to her mouth. She put it down again and looked about to burst into tears.

'That's not fair, Chris.'

Chris was immediately sorry for blurting out his thoughts and stared bleakly at his mother. She managed to control herself however, and the promised flood was averted. They ate the rest of their breakfast in silence.

As Sally was driving him to school, Chris said, 'Mum, I want you to teach me to dance.'

She glanced sideways at him. 'You're a good dancer, I've seen you.'

'No, I mean old-fashioned dancing. You know, ballroom stuff.'

She raised her eyebrows. 'You want to learn ballroom dancing? I'm not sure I'm that good myself. I can waltz and foxtrot – we learned that at school – but I'm not sure I can tango . . .'

'The waltz will do. Just teach me to waltz, will you? I know you're OK at it. I used to see you messing around with Dad sometimes. Will you?'

'Is there a special reason for this sudden urge? You're not going professional, are you?' she said jokingly.

'Don't make fun of me, Mum.'

'Oh, all right, grouch. Yes, I'll teach you to dance, if you really want me to.'

Chris said thanks and settled down into his seat to watch the open frosted fields go by.

In the playground, before classes began, Chris ran into Jason Swan. Swan glowered at him, letting

186

him know that all was not forgiven or forgotten between them. There was still a score to settle. The fact that it might never be settled and that life might thrust them both apart just as easily as it had brought them together was no consolation for the moment.

We're like sticklebacks in a jam jar, thought Chris, trapped in this school together. We don't want to be here, we don't like each other, but there's nothing we can do about it except swim around each other and wait until we get let out. There was not long to go, in fact, before they could go to sixth-form college.

For the rest of the day, when he wasn't busy, Chris thought about Emily and his feelings for her. It seemed he was never going to see her again and that hurt him badly. The thought that she was gone from him for ever gave him physical pain. He spent hours trying to contrive some scheme for seeing her again, but every idea he came up with seemed flawed and hopeless. Twice, he made the trip on his bike to a point as near to the farm as he dared go, without success. After that, he could do nothing but hope to discover, through Tom, what might be happening to the whole family.

18

The social services' case conference was held, with both parents present, and despite his great anger at being treated like a criminal James Craster behaved with dignity. To his consternation Hannah's friend Edith, their school inspector up until now, was not there to support them. The education authorities had sent a Mrs Patel.

James and Hannah Craster were told that the case conference was to decide whether the children were to be placed on the At Risk Register, if it was felt that there was a possibility of future physical or emotional abuse. A vote would be held amongst the specialists present, including the police, and the majority decision would prevail.

'How do you look on your actions *now*, Mr Craster?' he was asked.

'I – I feel I was quite wrong to use physical violence,' he muttered, looking down. 'I can see now that it's not the answer and I'm sorry for what happened. It won't occur again. I don't think anything would be gained by putting me in jail though,' he added. 'There's a lot of heavy work around the farm which can't be handled by my wife or the girls. It won't help my daughter if you send me away.'

The policeman present said it was unlikely they

would charge James Craster this time, though a warning would be issued.

Once the children themselves had been interviewed, and James and Hannah had convinced the meeting that no more harm would come to any of the girls, a vote was taken. The decision was not to put the children on the At Risk Register at this time.

'We shall monitor the situation closely,' said the senior social worker.

It was Mrs Patel, however, who insisted that Emily and Anne begin to attend school right away.

'Keeping them at home, even though they may be receiving an excellent education, has obviously arrested the social development of these children. I'm appalled to learn they've had no visitors, seen no other children but each other, and are deliberately kept in ignorance of the nature of the modern world. I understand they were visited by a school inspector and a doctor, but neither of these people seemed to know that the girls did not visit the mainland. I suppose each of these professionals was concerned with their specialism – education on the one hand and medicine on the other – but it still seems to me to be gross negligence . . .'

The social worker interrupted with, 'It may be that the professionals in question would assume that, since the girls were bright and healthy, all was well. It probably didn't occur to them to ask if the girls went to town at all.'

'Well,' said Mrs Patel, 'the damage has been done now, but I still think a few enquiries should be made.'

James Craster said in as pleasant a voice as he

189

could muster, 'You're Indian, aren't you? Well, we here in Britain . . .'

Mrs Patel replied, 'I was born and raised in Essex, Mr Craster, and I'm as British as you are, thank you very much. But let me tell you this – it wouldn't have mattered if I was born in the Punjab and had arrived off the plane yesterday. I'm a fully qualified educational psychologist and I think I know when children have an arrested development.'

James Craster wilted under her stare and wisely said no more.

Charlotte was told later by her mother that, since she was over sixteen, she was to be given the choice of remaining at home, or going to a sixth-form college. Charlotte said, 'Oh, Mamma, Papa, I'd much rather remain at home, if you please.'

Charlotte did not fear her father's wrath, because she never did anything to arouse it. She could see now that he had been very wrong to hit Emily but she could not condemn him. It was not up to her to do so. She had been horrified on the drive to town in the trap, by the number of people she saw in the streets, by the volume of the traffic on the roads, and by the general hustle and bustle of a thriving market town. The smells made her sick and the sights and sounds were terrifying.

'Everything is so ugly,' she whispered to her mother. 'Dirty and ugly.'

She saw nothing of beauty in the scenes, even where there *was* beauty. All she saw was the litter and trash in the gutters, on the pavements and roads. The odour of fumes from vehicles made her feel faint. People seemed angry and hostile, moving quickly from one place to another, having little

190

regard for other pavement users. Their mode of dress, their language, their physical appearance, all these aspects of the people from the outside world startled and upset her.

And finally, worst of all, they stared at her.

It was horror of the outside world that kept Charlotte from joining Anne and Emily. She was almost an adult. She was also more sensitive than her sisters. Raised in captivity, Charlotte was like a creature in a zoo. The thought of being thrown out into a jungle was abhorrent to her. There was nothing out there she wanted, not even a relationship with a man.

'No,' she said, without any hesitation, 'I should prefer to stay on the farm, if you please, Mamma.'

However, in his arrogance, James Craster took her plea as an affirmation of his methods.

'Charlotte,' Craster told his wife afterwards in private, 'is the only one of my daughters who understands what we're trying to do for them. Charlotte is a gifted, intelligent young woman with exceptional sensitivity and judgement.'

It was the first visit they had all had to the outside world as a family, but even those who wished to see it, like Anne and Emily, had little time to appreciate it. They sat in the back of the trap while Dan Selby drove Chervil, staring at the person opposite. If the girls tried to move their heads to look at some interesting object or person, James Craster would snap at them to mind their manners. The whole journey was tense for every member of the family. Emily kept her eyes open in case she saw Chris, and Anne managed to sneak a look at the wonders around her from time to time, but

Charlotte remained as rigid as a statue, deliberately ignoring a world she had discovered to be hurtful.

The family returned to Haworth Farm in a morose mood.

Emily was of course the renegade and was treated with cold civility by her father. The warning he had received, about emotional abuse, had completely passed him by. He had little understanding of such a term.

'I'm so dreadfully disappointed in you, Emily,' he told her out of her mother's earshot. 'You have failed me in every way.'

Coming from such a bigoted and narrow-minded man, this should not have worried Emily, but it did. He was her father and she needed his understanding, support and love, all of which he had withdrawn from her. She needed it especially now she was facing a traumatic change in her life: one which filled her with misery and terror. She needed his reassurance.

Instead, he told her he had never really been satisfied with her progress as a student, so perhaps it was as well she should join the riff-raff in the schools to attempt to complete her education. Emily felt isolated and unhappy. She had no wish to join the 'riff-raff' and wanted to stay at home like her sister Charlotte.

'You're not being fair, Papa, really you're not,' she sobbed.

'You should have thought about *fair* when you smashed our world apart,' he said quietly. 'Now you must reap the harvest of your indiscretions.' He slammed the door to her room behind him as he left.

Anne did not seem in the least worried about going to school, but neither was she excited either. Her expression, on being told what she must do, was quite devoid of any emotion. She was the baby of the family and even James Craster did not like to upset his youngest daughter.

Hannah said that Anne would probably spend more days ill at home than she would at school, considering she was such a delicate and sickly child.

Anne never revealed how she felt about going to school, but she was Emily's only comfort. The two of them sat on Emily's bed, the night before their first schoolday, hugging each other and crying, while Charlotte read Wordsworth's 'By The Sea' in a soft, calm voice. Anne always cried when Emily or Charlotte wept, so this display of emotion was no indication to anyone what was going on inside Anne's mind and spirit.

The two girls were to attend Crouchside High School for Girls. They had bought their uniforms. There had been interviews with the headmistress, Ms Mackleton, who promised the girls would be well looked after. They would be in separate years of course, but teachers would be informed of their unusual upbringing to date. Every effort would be applied to make sure they were not teased or taken advantage of because of their quaint behaviour and manners.

'Of course, we can't eliminate teasing *completely*,' Ms Mackleton had said, 'but we'll do our best. We have Chinese, Caribbean and Asian pupils too, who sometimes have different cultural backgrounds to the local girls, so we're well used to dealing with this kind of problem.'

Their first day at the school the girls were driven in the pony and trap to the bus stop, accompanied by their mother. Emily again felt sick on the bus, but surprisingly Anne was fine. The youngest Craster stared with interest out of the window at the wonders of the modern world and took them all in as if she were on a sightseeing tour of Egypt or India. To her this new world was a fascinating exotic place that captured her imagination rather than scared her.

Hannah took them all the way to the school gates where she handed them over to the playground teacher. Anne was introduced to a girl in her year and Emily to a girl in Year Eleven, who had been told of their unusual background.

The girl who was looking after Emily said, 'Hi, my name's Shanie – Chantal Turner, but everyone calls me Shanie. I'm s'posed to be looking after you. I'll get you to meet some of my friends later, but Big Mac said it would be best if it was just me at first.'

'Emily Craster,' said Emily, extending a trembling gloved hand to shake that of the other girl. 'How do you do?'

Shanie shook the proffered hand with some amusement.

'Big Mac says you've been kept locked up,' said Shanie. 'Wow, that must have been gruesome.'

Around them the hubbub of the playground – girls squealing and shrieking, girls chasing girls, girls at various activities, girls yelling to each other – was like a mad universe of stars spinning, rushing noisily around two quiet planets. Emily, whose heart was pattering with fear, had already

194

lost sight of Anne, swallowed by one of the constellations that formed, broke up, regathered and scattered throughout the void known as the playground. She swallowed hard, her anxiety threatening to stifle her, and tried to answer.

'Gruesome? Who – who is "Big Mac"?'

'Oh, *Miz* Mackleton, of course. Us girls call her Big Mac. She's all right – sometimes. You've got a funny accent, haven't you? You talk just like Helena Bonham Carter in *Howard's End*. Is that because you haven't met no one else?'

'Anyone else,' corrected Emily automatically.

'Yes, anyone else,' laughed Shanie, not in the least put out.

'By the way,' said Emily, shyly, 'do you know a boy called Christopher Hatchly? I believe he's at the school just along the road.'

Shanie said, 'Never heard of him. Emily, there are hundreds of boys at Crouchside.'

'Oh,' said Emily, disappointed.

At that moment the bell rang and the girls formed into lines before going into the school. Ms Mackleton was standing at the doorway as the girls filed past into the assembly hall. On seeing the familiar face of the headmistress, Emily smiled and said politely, 'Good day, Big Mac,' leaving the stunned head trying to rescue her bottom jaw. Shanie gasped and tittered.

Emily's feelings during assembly were confused. There was no doubt about it that she would have rather been at home. However, the situation was *interesting* and if one *had* to be at school, then it was obviously sensible to make the best of it. Emily had never been in a room with so many girls before, all dressed similarly, some of them stealing glances at her. She knew she was an oddity, but was not quite sure how to dispel that oddness in order to make herself less of a curiosity. The way she spoke seemed to amuse people, both what she said and how she said it, but it was not easy to alter her ways. They had been with her for fifteen years and were ingrained. At least, she thought to herself, I don't look any different from the others.

As the assembly came to an end there was a sort of hollow feeling inside her, with her wondering: *Will they ever like me? Will they ever know how I feel? Will they ever come to understand what it's like to be me?*

The first lesson after assembly was mathematics, a subject with which Emily had never really been happy. However, she found she could easily hold her own amongst the other twenty-five girls, some of whom found it impossible not to giggle whenever Emily was asked a question and answered in her precise diction. Several times the male teacher had to speak sharply to the rest of the class, to prevent a general uproar.

Once, he asked Emily how she had gone about her studies at home, and all Emily managed to get out was, 'When Mamma and Papa . . .' after which the class shrieked with laughter, almost reducing her to tears. However, the teacher soon restored order and she sat down again in her seat, poker-faced, refusing to give them any insight to her feelings. Emily *hated* being ridiculed and at that moment the only thing stopping her running through the doorway was the fact that she knew she would soon get lost in the streets surrounding the school.

After maths came chemistry, some of which Emily knew in theory, though she had never performed any laboratory experiments. During break, Shanie showed her the library, the toilets and locker rooms, the art room, the music room, and other parts of the school, pointing out various people on the way.

'That's Sheila Wilkinson,' whispered Shanie, as they passed a tough but well-developed-looking girl with a radically modified uniform. Her skirt was rolled up at the waist to reveal more leg. 'You want to steer clear of her. She's into everything – drinking, smoking and worse. She puts it about a bit among the boys, too. She leads a gang of tarty girls.'

'What are you lookin' at, you silly cow?' snarled Sheila as the two girls passed by.

'Nothin', Sheel,' said Shanie. 'Just showing Em around the school.'

'Huh!' snorted Sheila, her contempt for Emily obvious.

'What does she "put about"?' asked Emily, once they were out of range of Sheila's ear. 'And why are you a silly cow?'

Shanie gave her a funny look and said nothing.

After break, Emily was required to help dissect a frog in biology class. The class was separated into five groups of six pupils, each with a frog to cut up. She was probably alone amongst the girls in her own group in not finding the exercise revolting. Most of the girls squealed and made comments like,

197

'Urrggh, disgusting,' or 'I'm not touching it. It's all slimy and horrible!'

Sheila Wilkinson, in the group next to Emily's, made school history by suddenly shrieking, '*It's not dead!*' then grabbing a knife and hacking the corpse to bits in a mock frenzy. She was sent to Big Mac.

Cutting up the frog, for a farm girl who regularly gutted and skinned rabbits, was an easy task and not particularly offensive and Emily impressed the others.

'I'll do the cutting,' she told her group of five girls, and taking the knife she neatly slit the under-side of the frog and parted the two halves as if it were nothing but an overripe pear. Shanie was most impressed and kept referring to Emily as 'my friend Em' for the rest of the lesson.

One of the girls fainted in another group, as the distended belly of their own amphibian was pierced and a foul-smelling gas hissed out, overpowering even the odour of the formaldehyde. Emily had smelt worse from the creeks on a hot summer's day when the bubbles of decomposing shellfish burst in the mud. She was the one who walked to the bench and took the remains of the rotten corpse and threw it in the waste bin.

Her status had risen a great deal during the lesson, but fell during the next, which was English. Now she came into her own. Shakespeare's *Macbeth* was the subject, and Emily was asked what was the role of the witches.

She answered in a short speech and added, '. . . of course, when we look at the role of the witches, we have to examine it as part of the whole context of the nature of evil in *Macbeth*. For example, did

Macbeth murder the king, and others, because that murder was preordained by some supernatural force, or did in fact the witches' prophesies spur him on to do these wicked acts by making suggestions which appealed to his vanity and the intrinsic corruption of his ambition . . .'

There was a stunned silence, not because Emily was saying anything the girls had not been fed by the teacher, but because of the manner and confidence of the delivery: not faltering once; using copy-book English.

In a later lesson, when a question came up about Gray's 'Elegy', she recited all thirty-two verses of it, word perfectly, from memory.

Shanie was a bit miffed with her. 'You're showing us all up,' she complained. 'You better slow down a bit, mate. People don't like you to show off.'

'I wasn't showing off,' said the dismayed Emily. 'I was asked a question and I answered it.'

'Yeah, well,' said Shanie, whose mousy hair made her feel under threat from Emily's raven locks, 'you have to pretend you *don't* know everything, sometimes, or people will think you're a right big-headed so-and-so.'

At the end of the day Hannah was there to collect them and take them home on the bus. Anne managed to say she found school 'quite interesting' but there her confidences ceased. Emily felt exhausted and was still very unhappy, but she did not give her mother the satisfaction of knowing this and talked brightly about what had happened in lessons and how she was looking forward to tomorrow.

Hannah accompanied the girls for one week, then they began catching the bus on their own. Since all they did was take the bus to and from school, they actually still saw very little of the outside world. Outside the school gates, Emily kept a constant watch, looking out for Christopher. She did not know what she would do if she saw him, but she knew she would do *something*. Emily was not the kind of person to stand by while her love was taken away from her and cast to the winds.

19

Over the next few weeks Emily gradually became more used to her new way of life, though she never completely conquered her motion sickness and she made few friends at school. Shanie occasionally tried to introduce her to other girls but Emily had difficulty in understanding what was being said to her – the language of the playground was vastly different to that of the classroom – and having to ask people what they meant became embarrassing. There would be a rolling of the eyes and the word 'boring' was frequently used. Some girls were kind, but most kept her at a distance. She was 'weird' and 'creepy' and few thought the cultivation of her friendship worth the effort.

Teachers, on the whole, liked her. She was quick and responsive, intelligent, and above all *enthusiastic*. Teachers could forgive most things, but indifference was hateful to them. A girl who was eager to learn was to be treasured.

Emily had at last been introduced to television. The first programme she saw was a French lesson and afterwards, when the set had been switched off and girls were filing out of the classroom, she went forward and looked behind the television. Someone laughed, and a girl called out, 'It's magic, Emily!'

It was at least a week before she made the connection between soap operas and television. Every day the girls would be chattering about people she had never heard of, who seemed to live quite scandalous and squalid lives.

She would hear, 'Jody's havin' a baby by Wayne Ditson – she's only sixteen, after all.'

'Stupid, having a kid at that age. And you don't think *he's* going to stay around, do you? She must've bin mad, sleepin' with him at that party.'

'Well, I think he's reeeeeally sexy.'

Snatches of conversation in this vein left Emily both shocked and perplexed.

'If she's only sixteen, when did they get married?' she asked, partly out of curiosity and partly to enter the conversation.

The girls laughed and Sheila Wilkinson said, 'You're so bloody *boring*, Emily, it just ain't true.'

Later another girl called Debbie said, 'Don't take no notice of Sheel – she's all mouth really.'

Life at home did not improve for Emily. Her father continued to harbour a strong feeling of resentment against his middle daughter which was expressed in silence and rejection. He was coldly civil towards her, refusing to listen to Emily's pleas for understanding. She must have said 'sorry' a dozen times before she realised he was not going to accept her apologies and that he was determined to make her suffer.

Her mother tried to make up for this by showing her fondness, but Hannah was not good at demonstrating affection. In earlier times such love from Hannah to her daughters was taken for granted rather than displayed. Now it was necessary to show it, Hannah did so awkwardly, and it seemed to Emily, artificially.

Hoping to please her father one day, Emily went to show him a merit she had received for her work at school. She held out her book and said eagerly, 'Father, look at what the teacher says ...' She got no further. He simply glared at her and said haughtily, 'So, I'm no longer "Dear Papa", but "Father" now? These are the sort of manners you are prepared to adopt, are they? You have no affection in you, child.'

She saw then that it was hopeless and it seemed that he would never again praise her or give her credit for anything. He lavished all his compliments on his first daughter, Charlotte, who accepted them demurely. But at the same time she seemed to envy Emily and Anne without wanting to know anything about school, or what it was like in the outside world.

. Emily said to her once, 'Charlotte, I hope you didn't refuse to go to school because you actually *want* to go.'

'How do you mean, dear Em?' asked Charlotte, in her soft gentle voice, as she helped Emily with her homework one evening.

'I mean, dearest sister, I know you practise self-denial.'

Charlotte smiled and looked somewhat wistfully through Emily's bedroom window at the lights beyond the river.

'I should hate it out there, Em. I'm not like you and Anne. You are strong, both of you. I should be terrified if people were looking at me, studying me, trying to read the secrets of my soul. I don't fear the outside world, but I fear its inhabitants. Not that they would harm me physically, but I would *feel* them all around me, like curious and judging ghosts – do you understand what I mean, Em? It's the idea of them, being there, evaluating me. I imagine they would be able to look into my heart and see its stains and smears. I feel I wear my sins on my coat, like Haukyn in *Piers Plowman*.'

'Oh, Charlotte,' said Emily, dismayed, hugging her sister, 'you have no sins.'

Charlotte smiled sadly and looked at the four walls around her. 'Ah, but I have, dear Em, and I must keep them hidden out here, on the farm.'

Charlotte would say no more, but Emily sensed a deep, perhaps unfathomable injury within her sister, which was the root cause of her desire for renunciation and solitude. Emily stroked her sister's cheek with her fingers, trying to draw some of the sadness from her as if it were electricity and her hand some kind of device for absorbing unwanted power.

'Will you become a nun, do you think?' asked Emily. 'I think you would make a very special nun, Charlotte.'

Charlotte laughed and squeezed her hand, saying, 'Perhaps I shall? I shall get me to a nunnery. But what about Anne, Em? Hasn't she changed? No more delicate tummies, no more headaches, no more mysterious illnesses. Going outside has made her blossom.'

'I don't know about *blossom*,' said Emily, seriously, 'but it's as if she had been going to school all her life. I never once saw her in tears on the bus, as I was. She seemed to settle in just as easy as you please, making friends, coping with all those devices and machines out there. I don't know that she's *happy*, exactly, but she doesn't seem in the least worried about anything, does she?'

'Perhaps it's her age? And you know, Anne has always been a little more scheming than most people give her credit for, Em. I'm not convinced that Anne doesn't do just what she wants to do. She happens to like going to school, so she does it. If she didn't want to go, we should probably see another side of her. I love my little sister, very much, but of the three of us she is the most manipulative and knowing.'

'Do you think so, Charlotte?'

'I'm fairly certain of it, Em.'

Emily said, 'Well, good luck to Anne, then. I envy her. I wish I could be like that – not really needing anyone. She doesn't seem to, does she? I'm sure if Papa were angry with her, instead of me, she would just say, "Sucks to you." '

Charlotte looked puzzled and amused. '*Sucks to you*? What on earth does that mean, Em?'

Emily laughed. Some street talk was beginning to enter her vocabulary now. The day before yesterday workmen had arrived to paint the school and put all the girls into a twitter. One or two, like Sheila, had sent notes to them. Emily could not see what all the fuss was about, but she heard phrases like, 'Do you fancy the dark one? I do,' and 'He's gorgeous, the other one. I wouldn't mind a snog with him,' which Shanie was very happy to translate for her.

Emily said she didn't 'fancy' either man and

205

thought the idea of a 'snog' with one of them quite revolting.

'They're too old and they *leer*,' she told Shanie. 'Anyway, I have a beau. His name is Christopher.'

'Oooo-errrr,' said Shanie. 'Christ-o-pher. Nice. But don't let Sheila hear you calling him a *beau*. She's merciless, is our Sheel. Say guy, bloke – or even boyfriend at a pinch – but never say beau, Em.'

Emily filed that one away, aware of its importance.

She had accepted the role of assistant stage manager in the school's production of Noel Coward's *Blithe Spirit*. The drama teacher had tried to persuade Emily to take a part – there were not many pupils at the school with Emily's posture and clear diction – but the thought of performing in front of two or three hundred people filled Emily with absolute dread. So she became the ASM instead, which she was enjoying, especially since the stage manager was Shanie Turner.

A meeting after school had resulted in Emily missing her usual bus. She arrived at the bus stop to see Anne's worried face pressed against the back window as the bus moved away. She waved to Anne and tried to indicate that she would be on the next one.

It was a full hour before the next bus came and Emily had to stand in the drizzle under the cracked, dripping roof of the vandalised shelter.

While she was waiting impatiently, Crouchside High School for Boys disgorged its noisy inmates ⁀o the street some two hundred metres along the ⁀m the girls' school. There was an agreement between the two governing school boards that the boys' day would start and end later to prevent congestion on the buses. Thus the two sexes rarely crossed each other's paths, unless it was the result of a deliberate liaison. Emily knew that Shanie met a boy during her lunch hour sometimes, though Sheila Wilkinson was scornful of the girls who went out with 'schoolboys'. Sheila's boyfriend was nineteen and had a car.

At last Emily had an opportunity to spot Christopher among the boys. It was something she had been wanting to do for some time, except that it was a daunting task, wildly searching hundreds of boys' faces for the right one. Perhaps she had missed her bus unconsciously on purpose, to force herself through the ordeal?

The boys arrived at the bus stop, pulling each other about. One of them said, ''Ello, darlin', to Emily, then sniggered, while his friend cried in a very loud voice, 'Take no notice of him, he's a twit.'

Emily shrank within herself, feeling besieged and intimidated. Then at last she saw Christopher, walking past the bus shelter towards another stop further along. He was not looking in her direction at first but was talking to an Asian boy who was wheeling a bicycle. Finally Christopher looked up and stopped speaking to his friend in mid-sentence. He went scarlet. They stared at one another for a few seconds, then he said to his friend, 'I'll see you later, Ish,' and came over to her.

'Emma?' he said, as if he could not believe it was really her. 'It is you, isn't it?'

'Hello, Christopher,' smiled Emily.

'Hello, darlin',' said the young boy standing next to Emily and fluttered his eyelids.

Chris said to the boy, 'Less of your cheek, Braithwaite, or I'll clip your ear for you.'

Chris took Emily's arm and led her gently away from the queue, to stand by a garden wall.

'I've been trying to get to see you. Mum told me you'd started school. I came early a few days, because you get out before us in the evening, but I never saw you.'

'I've been looking for you, too. How are *you*? My father didn't cause a lot of trouble for you, did he?'

Chris said, 'He only wanted to wallop me – in *this* day and age. My mum told him where to go. He's bonkers, your dad. He was like a crazy man.'

Emily felt she ought to defend her father and said, 'He's not crazy. He just doesn't like the twentieth century.'

'Well, he's your dad, so you must know. Mine's bonkers too, you know. Drinks too much and gets stroppy. We've got something in common really. Hey, it's really good to see you. I've – I've been thinking about you a lot, you know.' He hesitated and then added, 'Actually, I thought about you all the time. I missed you, Emma.'

Her heart lifted when she heard these words. 'Have you – did you really? I've been thinking about you too. I told Shanie Turner you were my beau and she laughed. She said I should call you my boyfriend.'

Chris flushed with obvious pleasure at this and looked away for a moment, clearly embarrassed.

Emily said quickly, 'You don't mind, do you?'

Chris said, 'I'll be your beau, your boyfriend, or

whatever you like. I think you're really great, Emma. I like you a lot, you know? I think you're the nicest girl I've ever met. I love the way you talk – and everything.'

'I like you too, Christopher.'

To Emily, this was how it should be: two people exchanging their regard for one another. She knew love in its every form, as expressed by those who had experienced it, had sat and pondered on its mysteries for hours, days and years. She had studied love until she knew its every twist and turn. Emily thought love the only priceless thing in the world: the only thing worth sacrificing everything for, including liberty and life.

Her bus arrived and Emily quickly shook Chris's hand and said, 'Goodbye, Christopher. We'll see each other again soon, I hope,' then she ran.

On the way home she stared out into the gloom of the darkening flatlands with its solitary trees standing stark and mute on various corners of the landscape. A heron rose from a pool captured by the land when the sea was driven back by the Dutch engineers who had helped build the dykes in a previous century. Its grey form melded with the dark greyness of the sky and the earth where they moved into one another without a definite horizon. It was a moody scene.

Emily saw only beauty and drama out there.

At home she explained her lateness with her head held high. Her father made some fatuous remark about the unreliability of *schoolgirls*, a term he used scathingly, and her mother shook her head and sighed. Luckily, Anne had primed her parents, so the incident was quickly forgotten, at least by the female members of the family.

Emily went to her room immediately after dinner. There were no gatherings around the piano, these evenings, not since she and Anne had homework to do. So Emily escaped the glittering eye of her father, to bury herself in her books, and in her dreams. Christopher had come back into her life and nothing her father said could alter her happiness.

PART SIX:

A Fever of the Mad

20

The girls had to get their own breakfasts before walking all the way to the bus stop from Rattan Island, because their mother was helping their father with the farm animals. Charlotte made some porridge and told them she would clear away the dishes once they had gone to school. Anne gobbled her porridge and said, 'Thanks, Charlotte,' before rushing upstairs to get her school bag. Emily ate a tiny amount then got her own books. She and Anne then left the house together.

As they walked, Anne said, 'I'm going to be a seagull today – floating on the waves. It's nice and peaceful just bobbing around on the water.'

'Good for you,' answered Emily, amused by her sister's imaginative games, yet unable to enter into them.

February had been flung away quickly by the winds of March, thrown like an unwanted calendar page into the past. The winds of the flatlands and estuary country were much more violent than those in other regions, there being no barriers. Emily and Anne hunched against the dyke, waiting for their morning bus, watching the birds being thrown over the sky.

The bus came and the girls boarded, each lost in their own morning thoughts. Emily stared out of the window, watching the marshes go by. On either side of the road reeds were being whipped back and forth by crosswinds, flogging the shallow creeks. It reminded her of King Xerxes of Persia, who ordered that the waters of the Hellespont be given three hundred lashes for destroying his bridges in a terrible storm.

Emily knew she was a product of her upbringing: she loved ancient history and loathed modern history. All her images of war were of glinting helmets, phalanxes of spears, and wind-powered warships, of brave men-at-arms whose loved ones waited in the vineyards and olive groves for the return of their knights.

Emily was both excited and anxious. She had agreed to meet Christopher Hatchly after school and deliberately 'miss' the bus so that they could spend some time together, even though it meant lying to Anne and to her parents. But she could see no other way of getting together with her own shining knight.

Chris had gone to school whistling 'Dixie', which in itself might have been cause for alarm had not Sally been more preoccupied than usual. She had not carried out her threat to get back with her ex-husband, mainly because Chris had behaved like a model citizen since her warning. However, Tom was becoming a nuisance to her and yet she felt he was too nice a man just to shrug off with a few words. She did not want to hurt him, but at the same time she did not want a new man in her life, not until she had got her divorce out of her system.

Chris got out of the car with, 'I'll be late home tonight, Mum – rugger practice. I'll catch the bus.'

'What rugby practice?' she asked, coming out of her reverie for a few minutes.

'You know – games. I'll see you about seven.'

'All right. Have you got some bus money?'

'Yes, I'll use my own. Don't worry.'

It was not often that Chris stayed on after school and never had he offered to pay his own bus fare before today, but Sally was less attentive to the world around her than usual and though some minor alarm bells rang she did not let them concern her for too long and quickly returned to her dilemma.

That evening Chris left school in such a hurry he brushed past his old enemy, Jason Swan, lightly knocking him on the shoulder with his bag. Swan turned and saw that it was Chris and his bottom lip curled. 'Whaddyou think you're on, Hatchface?'

'Sorry,' said Chris, subdued, not wanting anything to interfere with his meeting Emily. 'Wasn't watching.'

'Well, next time you're not watching, you'll get my fist in your face, even if I get chucked out for it, understand?'

Chris left Swan still muttering threats after him, to hurry across the road to where Emily was waiting. They gave each other a shy, breathless hello and then Chris said, 'Look, I've had a great idea. It'll only take us just over an hour to walk to a bus stop on the way to Barling. What do you say? We could be alone then, without this mob . . .' He indicated the hordes of boys coming towards them,

215

cans of drink and packets of crisps in their hands, yelling and calling each other names.

'Will I still catch my bus?' asked Emily anxiously.

'Course – just a bit later on the journey, that's all.'

He grabbed her hand and walked her away quickly, heading for the edge of town and the cross-roads to the country.

It took them only ten minutes to get rid of the residential district and then they were on the lane which led to Barling.

'You know,' Chris confessed, 'I didn't want to see you again that time when your dad came and threatened me, but I couldn't stop thinking about you. You're different from any other girl I know.'

'And you have many acquaintances amongst girls?'

'No,' he grinned. 'Not that many. But, you know, I *see* them around, I know how they act. You – you're so grown-up really, so mature. You don't muck about and giggle and all that stuff. It really gets on your nerves sometimes when you're trying to be serious with girls and they make fun of you.'

Emily said seriously, 'I should *never* make fun of you, Christopher.'

'And I like that too – the way you call me Christopher. You have such a nice voice.'

'I like the way you talk too, Christopher. You sound like a frontiersman in the Americas. I'm sure Mr Walt Whitman would have considered putting you in one of his poems.'

'Who's Walt Whitman?' asked Chris, not unhappy at being likened to a pioneer of the Old West.

'An American poet – a very fine poet. He wrote a volume called *Leaves of Grass*.'

Chris sighed. 'That's another thing, you're much more intelligent than me.'

'It's got nothing to do with intelligence,' she replied. 'It's simply an interest coupled with a good memory.'

The day had clouded over and towards its close the darkness came in earlier than usual, sweeping as a slow-moving shadow across the marshes. The wind was against them and this made the going harder than usual. Chris was used to walking and set the pace, striding along the bumpy grass verge by the ditches and hedgerows, putting a hand into Emily's own whenever a car came swishing around a bend, protective of her, enjoying the warmth of her touch, reluctant to let go again once the vehicle had passed.

Gradually, their pace became slower and slower, as Emily complained that she was getting tired.

'I'm not used to this cross-country hiking, Christopher,' she said. 'I'm sorry.'

He said it didn't matter, but was worried when they had to keep pausing for her to catch her breath. If they didn't hurry they would not be at the next bus stop in time and most drivers would ignore anyone between the stops.

'Maybe we'd better let you rest for a few minutes,' Chris said. 'Then we can put a spurt on.'

He looked around for a suitable place to sit, but there were no stiles or indeed any fences. There was a church, however, just a hundred metres along the lane. It was to this drab building that he guided the weary Emily. She was almost staggering with

217

exhaustion when they reached it. There was a car parked on the roadside verge just beyond the gates, but no driver in sight.

The church was set back behind some horse-chestnut trees: a square, dark Victorian structure with high windows. Once through the lich-gate there was a small churchyard with a few mouldy stones and twenty metres beyond that the church door, fronted by yew trees with their sombre green-ery. St Mary's was situated in the centre of a triangle formed by three farming hamlets, but had no other buildings in its immediate vicinity.

The church door was open and they went inside. Emily slipped gratefully into the last pew situated against the back wall, around the corner from the porch. Chris sat beside her, watching her anxiously.

'I'll be all right in a few minutes,' she said. 'I'm just not used to walking so fast for such a long way.'

'You'll be fine,' he said. 'But we mustn't miss the bus.'

Inside the church it was cold, gloomy and very dim. Chris found it a little spooky, but he said nothing to Emily, not wishing to frighten her. He simply stared towards the altar, some twenty metres in front, only the altar cloth vaguely visible.

While they were sitting there Chris was aware of someone coming to the doorway, standing there for a moment, then closing the door. They both heard the latch go.

Emily whispered, 'Who's that?'

'No one,' said Chris. 'Just someone shutting the door.'

They heard the sound of a car engine starting.

218

'Someone has a motor car,' said Emily, becoming very worried now about getting home. 'We could ask them if they would give us a ride to the bus stop, couldn't we?'

'A lift!' cried Chris, jumping to his feet.

He rushed to the door of the church and turned the wrought-metal ring handle, but it would not open. He heard the car driving off as he struggled with the latch, twisting the handle this way and that, pulling and rattling the heavy oak and iron door. It was a moment or two before he comprehended the enormity of their problem.

'We're locked in!' he gasped.

Emily climbed to her feet and came to his assistance. Together they battled with the stubborn door, hoping that they were just turning the handle in the wrong manner. But after ten minutes of wrestling with the latch it was obvious that whoever had been standing in the doorway, peering within, had not seen them and had unwittingly locked them inside.

The pair of them began yelling, as loudly as they could, hoping to attract some passer-by. It was unlikely however that anyone would be walking a country lane in the dark. Even cyclists were a rarity in the winter months. Also, the church was set back from the road, screened by trees, and their voices would be unlikely to penetrate the stone and oak, let alone reach the ears of someone on the roadway.

Cars swished by every so often, their lights glittering on the stained-glass windows, but Chris and Emily realised how impossible it was to attract any attention.

Both of them spent a good thirty minutes looking for the light switches, feeling their way around the cold stone walls, behind pillars, even in crevices in the brickwork, all without success. It was most probable, Chris said gloomily, that the switches were in the porch on the other side of the door, where they could not reach them.

'I'll see if I can find another way out,' said Chris in the now impenetrable blackness. 'Maybe someone left a window open or something?'

It was a forlorn hope. There was only one door to the church and the high windows did not appear to open at all. Chris wondered about smashing one of the smaller ones but they would have a climb to reach it and then a big drop on the other side. It was not a practical idea. He balked at breaking the huge window behind the altar, which would probably cost thousands of pounds to replace. They were unfortunately trapped.

To his relief and pleasure, Emily did not start to cry, but accepted the news calmly.

'If we're to stay here the night,' she said, 'we must settle in comfortably. I'm *very* tired, Christopher, so do you mind if I just lie down on a pew here and try to rest?'

'No, you have some sleep. I'll keep feeling around to see if I can find anything. There's a small steeple on this church – I'll see if I can find a bell rope. We could ring the bell to get someone here.'

While Emily rested on the pew Chris felt his way around the square room, searching for anything that might assist them to escape. He could not believe they were going to have to spend the whole night locked up. Surely, a search party would find them eventually? If only he had some matches, or could find some somewhere, he could light the altar candles. Then at least they could see. If they had candlelight they could wave it in front of the windows to attract attention.

He could not find a bell rope. From what he remembered of the outside there was no real belfry: just a stunted, squared, wooden spire coming off the end of the church. When he stood below the point where he believed the spire to be, he could find nothing resembling a rope. He tried standing on a pew and waving his arms about in the darkness above, in case the rope was tied up high out of the way, but was unsuccessful.

After a long fruitless search, he called out softly to find out where Emily was and went and sat near her when she answered.

'You dad's going to kill us,' he said simply.

'He won't be very happy about this,' Emily sighed. 'I'm a little frightened, I must admit.'

'Well, my mum's not going to be over the moon either. It's just the excuse she needs to get back with my dad – I told you they're divorced? He's a pain in the neck to live with, is my dad. Worse than yours, I'll bet. They'll all be worried sick, won't they? Probably think we've run off to London or something, knowing them. Well, we can't do much about it, can we? I've done all I can. I'm sorry, Emma.'

'It's not really your fault, Chris. We're both to blame really. I suppose we should have obeyed our parents and not met again.'

'No way,' said Chris, emphatically. 'No way. No one can tell us to do that. It's not right.'

Emily said, 'We should not be in this quandary if we had obeyed them, though.'

Chris said, 'But it's not the end of the world, is it? We're not in any danger and we've done nothing wrong. It was an accident, getting locked in here, but it's definitely not the end of the world. They'll be upset, but we can't help that. I'm not going to feel guilty over something I couldn't help.'

'But if we hadn't gone for the walk?'

'So we went for a walk, so what? If we'd gone to a rave and bombed out on Ecstasy, or got drunk on whisky or something, they could complain, but going for a walk? That's just kids' stuff – and we're kids.'

Emily laughed softly and told him he was masterful, which made Chris laugh. He *was* worried by the reaction they were going to get from the adults, but rational consideration of the events told him they really had nothing much with which to accuse the pair of them.

They had done nothing wrong.

'I've got a rotten exam tomorrow,' said Chris. 'I hope they find us before then. I don't want to miss it.'

They talked in whispers for some reason, for an hour or three, the time going by so slowly it seemed that worlds must have been born, lived out their time, and perished.

'What do you think of your school?' asked Chris. 'Is it what you expected?'

'I don't really know what I expected, but it was quite a shock. You'll probably laugh at this, but what bothered me the most was the sharpness and hardness of everything. What I mean is, I pictured school as a sort of small, dusty room, with the light coming in bright-moted shafts through a dirty window, and a coal fire behind the teacher, warming her but no one else.

'I pictured worn, old, softwood desks, rounded with age at the edges, discoloured and stained with ink, initials carved into their tops. There would be rickety chairs to sit on, the wood browned by time like these old church pews. I thought the pupils would sit in rows, facing the front, where the teacher stood by a blackboard. There was a dingy softness to everything: a sort of mellow roundness.'

'Dickens,' grinned Chris.

'I suppose so. But what I found were bright lights, Formica-topped tables, sharp lines and hard edges, everywhere. Pupils milling around during a lesson, exchanging ideas, sometimes working in groups, sometimes alone. It was totally, totally different from what I imagined . . .'

Eventually tiredness came upon them, strong enough to defeat the miserable chilliness put out by the stone walls and floor. There were longer gaps between their questions and answers, until finally both fell silent, simply staring into the darkness.

They tried to sleep and did so fitfully. The winter was still trapped inside the stone walls and it was desperately cold in the middle of the night. Chris was in an anorak and Emily in a thick woollen coat, but they still found themselves shivering. They huddled together, hugging each other for warmth, stretched full length near the front of the aisle. Their one comfort was in using hassocks for pillows.

Emily was too tired to think about her feelings too much, but she was mildly surprised to find she enjoyed being held by Chris and that a vague excitement went through her. Had she been more awake she might have decided these sensations were slightly improper, but instead she allowed them to wash gently through her body like warm seawater, captivating her.

21

Emily awoke with Chris half-sprawled across her. He was still asleep. The bright, low sun was shining through the altar window illuminating the figure of Christ on the cross. Jesus had His head to one side, looking down on the pair, as if in great disapproval. Emily stared at the stern expression on the face of Our Lord and decided He knew what had happened. He had been there, after all, the whole night, staring down on the pair as they lay together, wrapped in each other's arms.

She was at that moment engulfed by a fear so enormous in its implications that she felt as if she were drowning in it. Her head felt giddy as the idea of what she had done swirled around with her thoughts in a murky whirlpool. Her father – her father would be beside himself with rage. Perhaps he would not allow her into the house ever again, but turn her from the door, and where would she go? With whom could she stay? Perhaps, like Jane Eyre, she would have to wander the countryside, wretched and forlorn, until some kind person helped her or she died of exposure.

As Emily moved, colours rippled over her coat. She saw that the hues from the sunlit stained-glass windows fell across their horizontal forms. They were enveloped in holy pictures of lambs, shepherds, angels and ancient kings. Deep blues and reds of Victorian glass tattooed Chris's face, as he lay beside her on the long narrow oak pew. The pair of them had been temporarily dyed by hallowed tints cast down by God's eye.

There was the musty smell of old carpeting and damp plaster in her nostrils. She sat up and shivered involuntarily, partly because of the deep cold that had found its way into her bones, and partly because she was afraid. She reached under her coat and touched her midriff. It seemed normal.

She looked around her, at the interior of the church, and saw to her dismay that there was indeed a small bell. The cord for the bell, however, was wound around a cleat attached to one of the side walls. She and Chris had been feeling around in the air for the end of a *dangling* rope, but of course the cord would have been well out of their reach.

'Oh, my nose and cheek hurt,' said Chris, stirring beside her. 'I must have been pressed up against the back of the pew.'

He opened his eyes. 'Are you all right, Emma?'

'I think so,' she said. 'Something woke me.'

At that moment they heard the lock turning in the door and then the door opened. They climbed to their feet as a man in a tweed suit came in. He seemed only half-surprised to see two teenagers standing in the aisle of the church. He was obviously upset that they were there.

'I had a feeling,' he said. 'When I heard it on the local radio this morning – there was something in my mind about locking up last night. I don't know what it was, I just had a feeling that someone was

226

around. When I heard two children were missing . . . it's a good job I decided to follow my instincts. You might have been in here until Saturday, when the ladies come to do the flowers. We don't leave this church open.'

'Didn't you see us last night?' said Chris, rubbing his legs, trying to get some warmth in them. 'We just stopped off for a minute for Emily to rest. She got tired walking to the bus stop.'

'I'm sorry, most dreadfully sorry,' said the man. 'The vicar will be upset too. I'm just one of the churchwardens. I simply didn't see you. Normally no one comes in here – not casual visitors. It's not a pretty church and it's well out of the way. I'd been working in here and just stepped out the back . . . well, you don't want to hear all this. Let's get you both home.'

Emily could see the man was worried and though she felt angry and upset with him she was too concerned with her own condition to bring him to task. Instead she allowed herself to be guided up the aisle by Chris and taken out to the car. The man turned to Chris.

'You live at Paglesham, don't you? I think it best we take you home first, as it's nearest.'

Without waiting for an answer he started the car and drove them back along the lane they had travelled last night. It took only a few minutes to cover the same distance that had taken over three-quarters of an hour to walk the previous evening.

When they stopped outside the cottage at Paglesham, Emily saw a small, blonde woman come running out of the house.

'My mother,' murmured Chris.

As Chris climbed out of the car, his mother got hold of him and, to his obvious embarrassment, hugged him hard, before crying, 'Chrissie, where have you been? Is this Emily? Your parents are absolutely distraught, Emily. Oh, where have you two been? Did you run away to London? Were you eloping?'

'Aw, Mum, don't be daft,' said Chris, squirming out of her arms. 'It was a mistake. We got locked in a church.'

Emily could see that Mrs Hatchly had been distraught too. Her eyes were red, with dark patches underneath them. Her hair was badly combed and hung in wisps over her face. There were creases in her clothes, which she had been wearing the whole night. Her complexion was grey and pasty. She still seemed more concerned than angry.

'We couldn't help it, Mrs Hatchly,' said Emily quietly. 'It was a most innocent mistake.'

'My name's Brampton,' said the man, speaking for the first time to Chris's mum. 'It was me who locked the church. I didn't see them. No one ever comes there, you see. I just locked it without thinking – at least, I glanced in, but it was dark inside and there was no reason for anyone to be sitting in the dark. Then this morning I got to thinking . . . I am most *dreadfully* sorry, Mrs Hatchly.'

'We just stopped to rest for a moment. I was walking Emma – Emily to the bus stop. She got very tired and we just stopped for a minute to let her get her breath back. She's not used to walking, are you? We were only in there for a minute when we heard a car start up and we found we were locked inside. It was flippin' cold, too.'

'All right, all right,' said Chris's mother, holding her head for a minute. 'It's not a catastrophe, after all. We'll sort it all out later. Your father's out scouring the London railway stations, Chris. I'd better call him – and the police – and the radio station. Come on in, we'll get you to bed.'

'I can't go to bed,' announced Chris. 'I've got an exam today. It's important.'

Chris's mother said, 'You can't go to school . . .'

'Mum,' said Chris in a determined voice. 'Nothing terrible happened. All we did was sleep in a church all night. I've had worse sleeps on Scout camps. I know you've been worried but I want to go to school. You've been imagining the worst, but it wasn't like that. We haven't been murdered and it's been no big deal. I just got a bit cold, that's all. I'm just going to go in, get a bath to warm up, then get to school – all right? I don't want to miss my exam.'

With that Chris said, 'Bye, Emma, see you later.'

'Goodbye, Christopher,' she replied, feeling he had failed to confess the most important aspect of their experience together. Perhaps, thought Emily, he's going to tell his mother in private? To Chris she said, 'Forgive me for having been so much trouble to you. I hope your exam goes very well today. Goodbye, Mrs Hatchly. I am sorry to meet you in such distressing circumstances.'

Chris's mother gave her a wry smile and reached in the car and squeezed her gloved hand. 'You seem like a nice girl, Emily. Under normal circumstances I would consider Chris to be lucky to have such a girlfriend. Would you like me to come with you and see your parents? Help you explain?'

229

'No, you have your telephone calls to make.'

Chris's mother sighed. 'That's true. The world and his wife is out there looking for the pair of you. I have to say I've had your father screaming at me half the night, calling me all sorts of names . . . well, that's not your fault. I do hope we see you again. I really mean that.'

'Thank you, Mrs Hatchly.'

Mr Brampton said to Emily, 'We'd better get going. Where's your place? Near Rattan Hard, isn't it?'

'Haworth Farm is on Rattan Island,' explained Emily, 'but if you take me to the hard I can walk the rest. You can't drive your motor car onto the island – the track isn't suitable for modern traffic.'

'Oh, but surely,' Mr Brampton argued as he drove away from the cottages, 'under the circumstances . . .'

'Under *no* circumstances, I'm afraid,' Emily said.

When they reached the hard, Mr Brampton insisted on accompanying Emily to the farm. Like Chris's mum, Emily's mamma came running out of the house. When she reached Emily she stopped short however, standing there in front of her like some predator, her fingers curled like claws.

'Where have you been, child? Were you with that boy?'

Mr Brampton said awkwardly, 'They were locked all night in the church, I'm afraid. It was my fault really. I didn't look hard enough when I came to closing up . . .'

'Yes, thank you very much,' snapped Hannah. 'You can go back where you came from.'

230

Mr Brampton's head shot back and he looked affronted. 'I beg your pardon?'

'I said you'd better get out of here, before my husband comes back. He has a fierce temper. If you had anything to do with helping these two rebellious children stay out all night, then be prepared for trouble.'

Emily could see that Mr Brampton was extremely indignant: aghast that he should be thus accused. 'I'm sorry, madam, but you don't understand. It was an accident . . .'

'Accident or not, it would be better if you left,' said Hannah, clutching Emily's arm and pulling her towards the house.

Emily allowed herself to be hustled up to the house and into the parlour.

Both mother and daughter watched through the parlour window as Mr Brampton shook his head slowly and then made his way back down to the ford. When he was out of sight, Hannah turned white-faced to Emily and said, 'Your sisters are up in their rooms. I don't want their ears defiled by your wicked escapades. Now tell me, what happened – and if you lie to me, child, you'll be very sorry later on, I assure you, social workers or no social workers.'

There in the parlour of the house Emily fell to her knees. Already under great strain, her mother's bitter tone made her guilt unbearable. Overwrought, and in a fit of trembling, Emily burst into tears and confessed to her mother, telling her the worst. Her voice was distorted by her emotional state, hardly even intelligible, and only a mother or someone very close would have been able to inter-

231

pret the meaning of them. The news made Hannah go very red at first, then a deathly pale. Finally, Hannah placed her large hands on the crown of her daughter's head while Emily was still speaking, as if she were trying to ward off some terrible divine judgement.

'Oh God, no,' she groaned. 'Not this – dear God.'

While she was in the process of revealing her sin to one parent, the other strode into the room, having been out searching all night. He stood there, stock-still, as she spoke, hearing the words coming from his daughter's own lips. When she dared to look up, Emily saw her father's face. From his expression an onlooker would have thought he was hearing a notice of execution being pronounced upon one of his family.

He asked in a barely discernible whisper, 'What was that? What did you say, child?'

'*Oh, Papa, I'm going to have a baby,*' Emily said tragically.

James Craster let out a cry like an animal in pain and turned towards the door.

Hannah stood up and shouted, 'James, wait!'

He ignored her, rushing blindly from the house, his flat cap falling to the ground as he raced down the cockleshell track to the hard. Not stopping to pick it up he continued running to where the taxi that had brought him home was turning around, preparing to return to Southend.

Emily saw him fling open the back door to the vehicle and jump in.

Then the taxi drove away.

Hannah turned to Emily. 'Oh, Emily, now see what's happened, you thoughtless girl. You won't necessarily have a baby, whatever you and this boy have done together. You could have kept that secret from your father. You silly child . . .'

Emily stared miserably up at her mother. 'But I *will* have a baby for certain, Mamma. You told me exactly how it would be.'

Hannah looked at her daughter long and hard with a strange expression on her face. 'Just exactly – exactly what *did* you and this boy do together? Tell me the details. Everything.'

'Why,' said Emily, 'we lay down together in the sight of God – so there *must* be a baby, mustn't there, Mamma?'

'Is that all? You didn't do anything else? He didn't touch you? You didn't – you didn't take off any of your clothes. You didn't *undo* anything?'

Emily was deeply shocked. 'Oh no, Mamma, that wouldn't have been proper. That would not have been proper at all, would it? We – were were fully clothed the whole time. I didn't undo a button, nor remove a stitch. But we lay by each other on the pew, for warmth, you see. It was so dreadfully cold. It was only in the morning, when I saw the picture of Jesus on the window looking down on us, that I remembered what you said about babies.'

It was Hannah who started to cry now. 'Oh, my dear child,' she said, hugging her daughter. 'My dear child. You're not stupid. How did you think it would happen?'

'Well, of course, something passed between us in the night, while we slept. Something from Christopher's spirit passed into mine. Isn't that how it happens, Mamma? Isn't it?'

22

When the first break-time came Chris gratefully left the classroom for the playground. His mind was buzzing through lack of good sleep. His history exam was not until eleven o'clock, so there was still time to revise dates and events in his mind, going over them parrot fashion. He walked around the edge of the playground with Ishwinder while they tested each other.

'The Corn Laws,' said Ishwinder, despairingly. 'I hate the bloomin' Corn Laws.'

Overhead the sky was purple-black, threatening a huge downpour. Great water-towers of cumulus rose from a thick cloud base, ready to release their load. Solitary birds were crossing the space between earth and cloud, rapidly seeking shelter from the oncoming storm.

'What are you two burbling about?' said a sneering Jason Swan, as they passed him. 'This exam's a doddle.'

Chris thought it would be nice if, as comics and books often depicted, all bullies were also dimwits. This was not the case with Jason Swan. Swan was one of the brightest boys in the school and seemed to have a brilliant memory.

Chris said, 'We're not all brain-boxes.'

'That better be a compliment, Hatchface,' said Swan in a dangerous voice.

At that moment there seemed to be a commotion going on in the playground. A man had entered by the front gates and was striding around in a kind of frantic search, staring this way and that, as if looking for someone. The teacher on duty was on the far side of the school, where the playground melted into the playing fields, and he came walking towards the intruder to find out what was the matter, but there was no urgency in his step. It was then that Chris recognised the intruder and was startled enough to cry out his name.

'Mr Craster!'

At the sound of his name Craster turned towards Chris and the man's eyes widened. There was a wild and terrible darkness in those eyes, set in a savage face, which frightened Chris. It seemed that Craster had been tipped over the edge into insanity. The farmer's normally brown complexion was the colour of dough and there were black creases, almost like deep bruises, across his frowning brow. His nostrils were red and flared like those of a snorting bull and his lips were drawn back revealing his teeth.

Chris turned and began running away.

Chris had only covered about ten paces when he felt himself gripped roughly by the shoulders and wrenched round. He was face to face with the twisted mask of the farmer, whose rage had robbed him of all sense and reason. Strong hands went in a stranglehold around Chris's throat.

Chris tried to shout, 'Leave me alone!' but nothing came out but a gargled, unintelligible noise.

Craster snarled, 'You little fiend! You nasty little swine! Rape my daughter, would you? I'll choke the life from you. I'll throttle you like a wild animal . . .'

At that moment the skies opened up, the threatened downpour arrived, and everywhere was awash.

Dimly. Chris could see the distant teacher break into a run, but he was over two hundred metres away. The heavy rain slowed the teacher's pace. Visibility dropped almost to zero. A sweeping wind blew stinging raindrops into Chris's eyes as he kicked and fought against his assailant.

Chris tried to pull the hands away but they were like steel claws. It was impossible to prise them open. The world darkened around him, as the storm lowered itself upon the earth. His neck was dreadfully painful. His head tingled around the base. There were bright lights, like white sparks, coursing in front of his eyes. He felt his life slipping rapidly away from him as the farmer stemmed the blood to his brain.

Then suddenly the hands were gone. Chris choked and coughed, gulping down air which hurt his bruised throat. Already on his knees he fell forward, his hands outstretched to stop himself from crashing onto his face. The lights in his eyes danced away now, gradually clearing. When he looked up he could see Swan standing with bunched fists over the prostrate form of Craster, threatening to hit the farmer again if he got up.

The teacher and Swan took Craster away, the farmer going limply and bemusedly with his captors. Ishwinder and another pupil helped Chris to stagger to the school where a second teacher took him in hand. An ambulance was called and Chris was whisked off to the casualty department of Southend General Hospital. Sally was called and she arrived just twenty minutes later.

There was of course a lot of fuss at first, which Chris wished would go away. Teachers, police, just about everyone was asking him questions. Even the local press came, but Sally soon sent the young hopeful reporter packing. Finally, Chris was allowed to go home. The police said there would be charges brought against James Craster, who was now in custody.

Later, Chris and Sally talked about the incident. Chris was still in a state of shock, but Sally had to know the answers to certain questions.

'He said something about me raping his daughter,' said Chris. 'He's mad. Me and Emily didn't do a thing.'

'You're positive about that?' asked Sally.

'Mother, I would know, wouldn't I?'

Sally replied in a puzzled tone, 'I just wonder why Emily would accuse you of such a terrible crime. Why would she do that? She must have done, for him to go rushing to the school and try to strangle you.'

The answer to this question came shortly afterwards, when Sally received a telephone call from Hannah Craster. She said she was at the police station and wanted to know if Chris was all right.

'Yes,' said Sally, 'no thanks to your husband. He could have been killed.'

'I'm sorry,' said Hannah Craster. 'I'm so dreadfully sorry. I know the children didn't do anything, but you see . . .' and she told Sally what had happened, how Emily in her ignorance thought she was pregnant, because she believed something *had* taken place when the two of them were asleep on the pew.

'It appears that my daughter,' explained Hannah in a broken voice, 'my *daughters* believe the act of – of procreation to be a purely spiritual thing. I'm afraid it's what I inadvertently led them to understand. I tried to emphasise that side of the act, you see, to give them some moral base on which to build a lasting, loving marriage. Unfortunately, I somehow neglected to teach them that there is a physical side to it as well . . .'

'It could happen to any parent,' lied Sally, feeling the woman's distress even over the telephone. 'We get embarrassed when it comes to explaining that side of things.'

'Such a dreadful thing to happen,' said Hannah, and Sally could hear that the woman was in tears now. 'I'm so sorry your son was hurt. Please try not to be hard on my husband. He only wanted the best for his children.'

Sally replied that she would try not to bear any lasting malice towards James Craster.

'It's a little early to be able to forgive and forget though,' said Sally, 'and the matter *is* in the hands of the police now.'

The telephone call was upsetting, but Chris's teacher David Gates arrived shortly afterwards to ask Sally if he could do anything to help. To his and her own embarrassment she cried on his shoulder. Jack was away at a conference and Sally was secretly glad about that. Jack would have condemned just about everyone involved, which would not have helped matters in the least. David Gates was simply full of sympathy and support, with no conditions attached to his role as a counsellor.

When Chris returned to school the first thing he did was walk up to Jason Swan and thank him for saving his life.

Jason Swan glared at Chris. 'You don't think I did it for *you*, do you? I couldn't care less if you dropped down dead now, Hatchly. I did it because *I* rule the playground – *me* – not some half-baked farmer from Rattan Island. I say what goes and what doesn't go . . .'

Chris shook his head slowly and walked away, realising that things between Swan and himself would never change, no matter what happened.

As to the things between himself and Emily, Chris despaired for both of them. It seemed that fate had thrown them together quite emphatically, only to toy with them afterwards, allowing them brief periods of hope, then ripping them violently apart again. Each time the damage had been made worse.

It seemed that there was nothing left for them now, except to avoid each other.

Epilogue

Some months after the incident in the playground, Chris was preparing to go to a residential sixth-form college in the north of the county. After the attack by Emily's father Chris had knuckled under and had got down to doing some serious revising. Only just in time, this hard work had paid off. Now he knew what he wanted to do. He felt he wanted to get away from the south of Essex for a while to find himself a little. If all went well with his studies, he hoped to make it to university.

At one time, leaving for college would have been a good excuse to get away from Jason Swan, but even Swan had faded into the background of Chris's life in the past few months. Swan was no longer important, no longer a large and threatening force. He was simply an occasional irritation that would go away of its own accord eventually. Not that Swan was any less aggressive, but Chris had ceased to care about him.

Coming out of the school gates on a warm, pleasant evening Chris saw Emily Craster, standing quietly on the other side of the road. She seemed to be waiting for someone. He had not met her, to speak with, since her father had attacked him. It was not that Chris had anything with which to reproach her: they simply had not contacted each other. There was a kind of unspoken agreement between all parties concerned, that it was better to let matters rest between them for a while.

Since Emily's father had pleaded guilty to the charge of assault, there had been no need to involve the two adolescents in the court case, and James Craster was now undergoing six months probationary service.

Chris turned to walk to his bus stop, when he saw a flutter of a hand, and Emily called to him. 'Christopher?'

Chris paused in his stride. He looked across at Emily. It wasn't that he felt hostile, far from it, but he was naturally wary. Her father had scared him badly. Chris knew that the farmer would think very seriously before attacking him again, but the man was unpredictable and irrational. Finally Chris decided there was no harm in speaking with Emily and crossed the road.

'Hello, Emily.'

She smiled. 'Hello, Christopher. You didn't call me *Emma* for once.'

'Oh, that was just a – you know.'

'Yes, a pet name – no longer appropriate. I always wanted to call you Kit, but I thought you wouldn't like it.'

'I wouldn't have minded,' he said.

She smiled again, then her face was serious. 'First of all,' she said, 'I want to tell you how sorry I am for what happened with my father . . .'

He interrupted, embarrassed. 'Oh, it wasn't your fault. I'd rather just forget it. Honest. I'm off to a sixth-form college soon, so it'll all be history. What's happening to you?'

'Well, I hope to go too, in a little while, but I was thinking of studying somewhere abroad. Paris, probably. My French is quite good and I won't be so out of place there. All they will see is a plain little English girl.'

'Plain?' You're very pretty. Hey, how are your sisters?'

Emily appeared relieved that he wasn't upset with her about James Craster and her face brightened on hearing the compliment.

'Charlotte and Anne? Well, poor Charlotte still hasn't left the farm since her visit to Rochford. She says she would prefer to be with Mamma for always, and Mamma does need her, but I can tell she's unhappy. She doesn't like the outside world, but now she's seen it she's uncomfortable with the small tightness of her world on the farm, and I wonder what will happen to her when Anne and I leave home for good.

'Anne's doing very well at school. She says she wants to go to London when she leaves. Listen,' Emily said, changing her tone and speaking more quickly, 'there's to be a dance – a disco, they call it – involving both our schools. I expect you're going?'

He hadn't thought about it, but he said, 'Yes, I expect so.'

'Well, so shall I. My parents are keen that I should take part in extra-curricular activities – at least, the social workers are – and so I'm permitted to attend the – the end-of-year disco. I thought you might be going too and I wanted to speak to you first, to dispel any awkwardness between us. It would be silly if we were to bump into each other by accident at the dance and then go red with embarrassment, wouldn't it?'

Chris was once again quite impressed by Emily's thoughtfulness and foresight. 'I suppose you're right. Well, now I know, I shan't be bowled over backwards.'

Her lips twitched a little. 'Are you making fun of me?'

'No, no,' Chris said hastily. 'Of course not. In fact – will you save a dance for me?'

'Oh yes, *indeed* I will.'

The sight of her face lighting up at his request was enough to send him home afterwards in a deeply thoughtful mood.

When the night came for the dance, Chris dressed and went downstairs to the living-room. Sally was sitting there talking with her new boyfriend. He was a man about whom she was growing rather serious, and Chris liked him. It was David Gates, Chris's maths teacher, which might have proved awkward at one time, but since Chris was leaving it didn't seem to matter in the least.

'You're looking very sober, for a disco,' she said, staring at Chris as he descended the stairs.

'You mean the clothes? Oh, well, I'm getting older. Jeans and T-shirts are for kids.'

He had put on cords, a plain shirt and a jumper.

David said, 'Well, I must admit, that's unusually quiet.'

'I feel quiet,' said Chris. 'I feel placid and serene.'

This raised eyebrows but no further comments.

Sally drove Chris to the girls' school, where the disco was to be held. He asked her to meet him at

243

eleven o'clock. Then she drove away, leaving him to enter the building.

Emily saw him come through the doorway, then she quickly looked in another direction. Although she had been waiting for Chris to arrive she did not want him to know it. She had been half-afraid that he would not come, now that he knew she was going to be there. However, there he was, and she was happy to see him, though she didn't want him to know that, yet.

Sheila Wilkinson said, 'Breaking out a bit, eh?' and gave Emily's dress the once-over.

Sheila was dressed in red tights, black mini-skirt, low-cut red sweater and masses of hair gel and make-up. She had red plastic bangles on her wrists and huge red plastic earrings. Around her neck were some large black beads.

Emily had on a plain frock, which might have been a ball gown had it been a little fuller, flat-heeled shoes, and no make-up. It had been enough to get to the dance, without trying to get her mother to agree to a colourful outfit. She had managed to borrow some lip gloss from Shanie, which she had applied so carefully Shanie had told her it was almost invisible. 'You look as if you've just licked your lips a bit,' said Shanie, but Emily was satisfied with that.

Emily glanced out of the corner of her eye and saw that Chris had walked over to a bunch of boys and was chatting to them in an animated fashion. Then he went to the bar and got himself a Coke and some crisps and sat down. There he stayed for the greater part of the evening, sitting next to a boy

244

wearing a turban, who Emily guessed was Chris's best friend, Ishwinder Singh. At one point Chris said something to his pal, who looked across at Emily, smiled, and waved. She waved in return.

Chris had told Emily, and she had learned from other sources, that he was a good dancer. She had witnessed modern dancing at school, without the boys present, but now that the music was at ear-splitting volume, the strobe lights were flashing, and the bodies were twisting, writhing and jerking on the floor, it seemed like a nightmare to her. They even spun on their bottoms and went down on all fours like dogs.

She froze every time Chris moved a centimetre, praying fervently that he would not come across to her and ask her to dance one of those wild, athletic dances. She would have been hopelessly inadequate and would have made herself a laughing stock, especially with someone who was good at it.

The thump, thump, thump of the deep loud bass pulsed through her like a physical presence in her body. Emily felt that her soul was in the thrall of some savage god, demanding she make extravagant movements, insisting that she spring to her feet and jig and sway. Screaming singers, clashing guitars, searing drum rolls, all added to her excitement.

Finally, the boy behind the table, playing the records – the DJ, she understood he was called – said there would be 'a smoochy one' and advised one and all to grab their girlfriends.

Chris rose to his feet and crossed the room. He had not danced once, the whole evening, despite some of the girls asking if he would. Instead, it seemed he had saved himself for this moment. He stood in front of her, smiling.

'You look very nice, Emma. Could I have this dance, like you promised? You can waltz to it, you know. You once told me you could waltz.'

She beamed. 'Oh yes, thank you – Kit.'

He took her right hand in his left and placed his own right hand around her waist. Then he swept her out onto the floor, his steps a little stilted, but nonetheless in time with the music. Emily found it a little awkward, following rather than leading, but her movements were fluid and accomplished, though she was unused to the tempo of modern dance music. Together, the pair of them drifted over the floor, between the shuffling, smooching couples, for all the world as if they were completely alone on a ballroom floor. She had never felt so happy before in all her life.

When the dance was finished, Emily was feeling flushed. Chris saw her back to her seat and then sat down beside her, whispering, 'Your eyes are sparkling.'

'Are they?' she said breathlessly. 'I suppose they must be. I feel as if I'm sparkling all over. Oh, Kit, that was wonderful – and so lovely of you to wait until the music changed. You knew I couldn't do that other kind, didn't you? And where did you learn to waltz so well?'

'Mum taught me.' He grinned. 'I asked her to, after that first time we went for a walk. I wanted to impress you.'

'Well, you've certainly done that. It was marvellous. Look, Sheila Wilkinson's glaring at me. I do believe she's jealous. I hope she is. She should be. Oh, Christopher, are you really going away?'

'Yes, I am,' he said seriously, taking her hand in his, 'but I want you to promise to write to me. Will you?'

'Of course I shall – and perhaps one day?'

'Yeah.' He grinned again. 'Maybe one day they'll leave us alone and we can get to know each other properly.'

She was content with that. Very content.

Emily returned to Rattan Hard by taxi, taking her shoes off to cross the ford. As she approached the house she could hear the piano being played. She stopped for a while outside, listening to the music. Emily could tell from the playing that it was her sister Charlotte at the keyboard. The notes were delicate, rather than definite, creating an ethereal air, as if the player were not quite real, but had somehow been wafted in on the night breezes from some other world.

As Emily stood there she noticed that someone had come out of the barn and was standing quietly, also listening to the music. Emily saw by the light from the kitchen window that it was her father and he appeared to notice her at the same time.

The two of them remained perfectly still, listening to Charlotte, until the piece had finished and there was silence.

Emily said, softly, 'She plays beautifully, Papa.'

He stared her her, his eyes hidden in the poor light, then finally he replied, 'Yes, she does, doesn't she? Shall we go in and join them? Perhaps – perhaps you might recite a poem for us this evening,

Emily? What do you think? Your mother, she misses your recitals, you know.'

Emily realised her father was at last trying to make friends again. She suddenly felt a kind of infinite sadness at something which had been lost, which by its very nature *had* to be lost, like a child's belief in fairies, or Father Christmas.

'I shall do your favourite, Papa – Shelley's "Ozymandias".'

He nodded thoughtfully and together they went into the house, where Charlotte and her mamma were laughing at some outrageous joke dear Anne had brought home from school.